I0725677

HALCYON:
An Alien Scifi Romance

DEMELZA CARLTON

Copyright © 2016 Demelza Carlton

Lost Plot Press

All rights reserved.

ISBN-13: 978-1-925799-26-2
ISBN-10: 1-925799-26-3

DEDICATION

This one's for the man with the physics PhD who made certain I knew the nuclear weapons in this book could destroy the city.
I'm not sure I reassured him much when I told him I was counting on it.

ONE

On a planet far from home, a solitary siren sped through the wine-dark sea toward her quarry, swifter and more deadly than a long-extinct shark. Her target, a Human ship, lay becalmed in the waves. Almost as if it expected and awaited its fate.

Halcyon the siren paid no thought to the ship's passengers or crew as she hauled herself up the *Poseidon*'s anchor chain to the deck. She listened for one voice and one voice alone – a prisoner the Humans had taken. A civilian they had no right to take.

As she stalked the deck, she lifted her voice in song. Humans heard and fell into slumber. Those who already slept sank deeper still. Deadly music echoed along the passages as she passed, until she heard a pained gasp, followed by, "Halcyon, dearest, you should not be here!"

Halcyon wrenched open the hatch that was all that lay between her and her husband. Except that the man she beheld no longer looked like her husband, for all that he spoke with Ceyx' voice. The bloodied piece of meat strapped to a table before her didn't look like a man at all, let alone a living one.

"What have they done to you?" she whispered, reaching out to touch the man she loved.

The homunculus coughed, bringing up more blood, which he spat on the floor. "Tortured me for information, dearest. They think me one of them, and a traitor. My research – " He coughed again, more thickly this time. "My research is what they wanted. Human and Titan genetics. They are the same.

The same, dearest. We can breed with them and they with us. Worse, if they work out how to bestow Titan powers on their own, they will annihilate us. That is why they tortured me. I refused to experiment on them. To work for them. I will not be a part of – " A deep, hacking cough seized him, leaving him gasping for breath that he was unable to draw from the air.

An eternity passed in a moment, as Halcyon was forced to watch her husband suffocate to death, like a fish out of water.

Her blood boiled within her veins. Titans were violent, yes, but none would dare harm one of the Mer, let alone attempt to torture one. Not like this. Not knowing what one siren could do to thousands of them.

Halcyon scanned the room, her fingers itching to show them what she thought of such despicable tactics. Her gaze lighted on a slumbering Human, almost hidden under a bench. Sleep was a luxury he would never know again.

"Wake," she commanded him, first in her

language, then his own when she got no response. The ignorant Human didn't speak Mer, so she would speak in English, and in pain. Both languages he would understand before he died.

The man blinked, patting down his lab coat that looked so much like the one Ceyx once wore to work. No more.

Halcyon ripped the plastic name tag from the man's chest. "Get up, Doctor Claudius Tasker. Did you do this?" She pointed at Ceyx' corpse.

"The traitor wouldn't talk," Tasker grumbled.

"So you tortured him?" Halcyon demanded. "A doctor. A healer. You caused harm that killed him?"

"I had to. The traitor wouldn't cooperate," Tasker said.

His last words. Halcyon screamed, a wordless sound that didn't need words.

Tasker clapped his hands over his ears, but it was already too late. Blood streamed from his eyes and nose as Halcyon hit the precise frequency that made every blood vessel in his head burst. The man dropped to the floor, as dead as Ceyx.

But one life was not enough. Ceyx would not want his research to become widely known, especially among Humans. That meant destroying all knowledge of it on this ship. In data banks. On paper. And inside Human heads.

A bereaved siren's grief knows no bounds, and a siren seeking vengeance for murder would make her fury known. She was the storm no Human could escape.

Halcyon raised her voice again, louder than before, as she marched with gruesome purpose to the bridge. There, she found Humans sprawled all over the floor and the consoles, but she didn't need to wake them to find what she wanted. She had spent six years studying Human technology, as her husband sequenced their genetic code.

She turned on all the pumps, flooding the ballast tanks with seawater until it sloshed into the cargo hold and overflowed into the lower decks, too. She would send Ceyx to a fitting grave in the ocean depths, and all aboard the *Poseidon* would rest with him.

When she dived from the deck into the waves, the ship sat so low in the water she could reach over the gunwale with her hand. Not for long. The *Poseidon* sank beneath the surface, leaving only a single floating lifeboat to mark its existence. A lifeboat, where there was nothing but death.

And Halcyon, who would exact a siren's vengeance from all the Humans who had summoned the storm by daring to steal her husband from her, even as she cried an ocean of tears for his loss.

Neutrality was a luxury for other sirens who had not lost a lover to the barbarous aliens. Now, for the first time in living memory, a siren went to war.

TWO

Ten years. Ten long, hard years, he'd worked and waited for this. Ten years since the night the *Poseidon* sank, drowning all the family a teenage apprentice engineer had left. At the time, he'd thought the three weeks he'd floated in a lifeboat at sea were forever, vowing vengeance on the copper-coloured fish tail he'd glimpsed in the dark, swimming away from the sinking ship. Galen grinned at his own naiveté. War had wised him up quickly to the world he lived in, or the Altan system, anyway, as he stood on New Hope today for the first time, staring up at the soaring domes of his Colony home like all the other new colonists, Human and Titan alike.

Since the war ended, he'd gradually learned to see Titans as more than just the enemy. Four years ago, he'd have itched for a weapon at the sight of the family in front of him — shifters of some sort, he figured, given the fur some of the children sported, which couldn't be comfortable in this baking heat — but now he just felt a sort of aching envy. Not for the parents, but for the kids. He'd had a family once, and he would have liked to show his father how he'd turned his passion for tinkering with things into a career that put him in charge of managing the environmental controls of this incredible facility. His dad had never understood how Galen didn't want to be a doctor like him.

His mother…she would have admired the dome, for she'd had a technical bent that she'd passed on to Galen, but she would have been more impressed at the possibility of peace between Titans and Humans, cooped up in the Colony. If his mother stood by his side now, Galen might have been tempted to believe it, too, but peace was a pipe dream. As long as one Titan lived who kept on killing, there would never be peace between their peoples.

Halcyon. One Mer was to blame for so many deaths, including those of his parents, Claudius and Panacea Tasker. He'd been chasing the bitch for a decade, always too late to see any more than the carnage she left in her wake, but now he'd finally struck it lucky. To a terrorist like her, the Colony would be the ultimate prize, because destroying it would mean an end to peace. Through his contacts, he'd discovered that she was believed to be among the colonists, which meant if he signed up, he'd have five years to search for her. Five years where she couldn't get away. After that time, when she was as dead as his parents, maybe he'd be able to look at Mer without hating them. Maybe.

Staring around at the mostly humanoid crowd sweltering in the packed tunnel that led from the shuttle to the Colony, he wondered how the Mer would enter the Colony. Would someone wheel a huge water tank out of one of the shuttles, and drag it into the Colony to the Aqua Dome? He hoped to be inside by the time that happened. He'd only ever seen one Mer in his life and it had been her. If he saw the copper-coloured tail that had haunted his nightmares for a decade, he'd dive into that tank and try to kill her with his bare hands. Hardly a good start to what was supposed to be an experiment in peaceful, mixed-species living.

Mixed species...he'd heard rumours of a bonus the Senate would give to any couple who produced a mixed-species child. As if such a thing was even possible. Even if they were able to breed (which he strongly doubted – wasn't that what made a species a species? They could only breed with their own kind?), just the thought of wrestling a slimy, fishy-smelling Mer into his bed…and where did you put it? Did she have some sort of trapdoor in her tail, or did she spawn like fish, so all a guy had to do was squirt into a bathtub where she'd laid her eggs and…ugh. It was enough to turn Galen off sex for life. Sex with fish was bestiality, tits or no tits. Period.

He shivered, trying to forget her and just focus on the moment. He stood in a queue that stretched so far from the Colony entrance he couldn't even see it yet, but he knew it was there. They all did. Somewhere at the end of the line was a door that led to the hope of a better life. Hope hung in the air like humidity — a hot and cloying security blanket you believed with all your might would keep the monsters at bay.

Galen wanted to believe it. If his hunt for Halcyon meant that no other child would wake up orphaned by a war he didn't want and would never understand, then it was worth it. He'd do anything it took to catch her, because the end justified the means. Any means. As long as it resulted in her end.

THREE

Allie shivered as she stepped into the Colony. For the queues forming up down in the cargo bays, the warmth she'd found so welcome would be a catalyst for fights breaking out. Short tempers in the heat…she didn't envy the Watch today. Especially not with the shuttles vomiting their humanoid cargo out faster than the Watch could process them, poor people.

So Allie summoned her brightest smile for the woman wearing a freshly-pressed Watch uniform. "Good morning, I'm Allie," she sang out, holding out her bag for the customary search before the woman could ask. She began humming a cheerful tune.

"Violet," the woman said. She took Allie's bag and rummaged through the contents. After little more than a cursory examination, Violet looked up to meet Allie's gaze. "Who brings a bag full of chocolate as their only personal items for five years?"

Allie winked. "Someone who appreciates life's pleasures."

Violet's expression softened into a smile. "A woman after my own heart."

Allie became aware of an alluring floral scent that intensified. "And you smell…absolutely enchanting, Violet. You're a succubus, yes?"

Violet nodded curtly as uncertainty filled her eyes.

"I've never known one before, but I'd like to. Come visit me in the Arena Dome one day when we're both free, and I'll share some of my chocolate, if I have any left." Allie rattled off her apartment number to the surprised succubus.

"But…how do you know where you'll be staying? You don't have your accommodation assignment yet," Violet protested.

Another wink. "I was part of the team who did the final structural checks on the Colony. I got a peek at accommodation assignments before they were finalised. Anything goes wrong at your place, you'll know who to call."

Violet nodded and waved Allie on to the next Watch officer, a Human male who introduced himself as Henry. Several minutes later, armed with her new tablet and a map she didn't really need, Allie boarded one of the waiting aircars to zoom her to her apartment in the ring surrounding Arena Dome. This was the last time she'd see Metropolis empty. By tomorrow, the place would be bustling with activity as all the new businesses started up. She sincerely hoped there'd be a chocolate shop somewhere. Hmm, perhaps she should have chosen to live in the Nyx Dome, where the products wouldn't melt quite as quickly as in the Arena Dome.

Speaking of which…

The first thing Allie did when she entered her apartment was to empty the contents of her bag into the refrigerator. Even the concrete floor was warm underfoot in this dome – lovely. And she had a window to the outside, just like she'd requested. A window that stretched across the ceiling from one end of the apartment to the other. More than a lowly maintenance worker had any right to expect, but those who'd put in the extra time during construction had been promised extra credits for their efforts. She'd refused the cash in lieu of an apartment with a view. And what a view. She threw her head back and stared up at what looked like the whole galaxy. New Hope's barely-there atmosphere meant there was nothing to obscure her view of the stars. Beautiful. She couldn't wait to watch the night time show through her skylight. It had been a long time since she'd had the leisure to simply lie back and watch the stars.

Allie debated whether to lie on her bed and rest while she had a chance, or head back to the entrance to watch the new colonists arriving and help where she could.

Plus, she'd be on hand to deal with any maintenance requests. Other people might not start their new jobs until tomorrow or even next week, but like the Watch, Maintenance staff were on call the moment they set foot in the Colony.

She should probably activate her communications device now she was here, too. Allie had only a moment to register that she had four messages before her comm alerted her to an incoming call.

"Hiya, this is Allie," she answered breezily.

"Is this Maintenance?" a male voice demanded. "We've just arrived at our apartment and there's ice all over the floor."

Allie reached for her tablet. "Yes, sir, I'm Allie from Maintenance. Can you tell me your apartment number in the Nyx Dome, please?" She jotted down notes as he talked, shaking her head at the sloppiness of the staff who'd inspected Nyx Dome. She'd had a wager with Ira that her first call would be from Nyx Dome. When she felt she had enough details to head over to fix the problem, she said, "I'll be right over, sir. I'll have your ice rink uninstalled in no time." She terminated the call. Time to get to work.

Whistling, she summoned a skimmer and set off for the snow.

FOUR

After what felt like forever, but was probably only a few hours, Galen stepped into the cool air of the Colony.

"Put you bag here," a woman in a black Watch uniform instructed.

Galen slammed his bag on the table, folding his arms as he waited for her to conduct her search. He didn't know what she was so grumpy about. She looked and smelled fresh as a flower, while he'd been standing in the hot tunnels below the city for hours behind that family of shifters that stank of the worst kind of musk he'd ever smelled. He'd heard about skunks, but he'd thought they died out back on Earth. Evidently the Titans hadn't killed their smelliest species off. Just like they tolerated Mer among them, knowing what they could do.

The woman took her time with his things, removing everything from the bag and inspecting the lining before she replaced everything, one item at a time. Everything except one thing. "What's this?" she asked suspiciously, holding up the first device Galen had ever created.

He reached for it, scared she'd drop it, but she stepped back, keeping it out of reach. Galen's arms dropped to his sides. "Please be careful. That's my…it's a music player. When I was a kid, I made it out of spare parts from the ship, so I could listen to the old Earth music my mother brought over with them. Those are the earphones, so only I could hear it, and it wouldn't disturb my parents while they were sleeping." He swallowed the lump that had formed in his throat. "It's all I have left of my family. They were killed in the war."

Her eyes searched his, as if reading more than just what she could see. She gave a little nod. "What kind of music?"

"All the classics from Earth, my mother said," Galen replied, spreading his hands. "Want a listen?"

She allowed him to place the earphones on her head, and closed her eyes when the music began to play. She stayed that way for a long moment, before gesturing for him to remove the earphones, which he did.

"It's not bad," she admitted, her lips lifting in a tiny smile. "Did you really make that?"

Galen nodded. "It's pretty rough, and I could probably do a lot better now, but it does the job. Nothing like as complex as this Colony here, though. I expect this place will keep me too busy to build toys like this. I'm the environmental engineer, so it's my job to make sure everything here works."

"Not just yours. I met one of your Maintenance crew this morning. A very nice Titan." She grinned widely, then hastened to add, "Not that there's anything wrong with Human, of course, but…"

That made the Human-looking woman a Titan, too, Galen guessed. He knew it was rude to ask, but he wanted to know what kind of creature she was. He worried that she was one of the ones who could read minds, even despite the implant he wore that was supposed to prevent that, though he'd never had a chance to test its functionality until now. He touched the scar behind his ear for reassurance. Of course it was still in place. Whether it worked, though…

The woman's eyes turned cold. "You'll pick up your accommodation and work assignment over there. Stay out of trouble, Human." She pushed his bag toward him and directed her attention to the next person in the queue.

Galen received his accommodation

assignment and everything else he needed from a man he was almost certain was Human, but he still wouldn't have bet a single credit on it. Not even with the fifty thousand credits he'd been given when he accepted this assignment. If he made it through the duration of this strange social experiment in the Colony, he'd use his government payoff to fund his own company, inventing things. But that was more than five years away. After he'd completed the mission he'd been working on for a decade.

The Watch officer cleared his throat.

Galen realised he'd been daydreaming again. "Sorry, what did you say?" he asked.

"That one's headed to your dome. Take that aircar to your apartment," the man said, waving him away.

Galen squeezed into the packed aircar. The door slid closed behind him and the vehicle took off.

The trip was long enough for him to get a good look at his fellow travellers. A few

Humans, a grey-skinned man whose attention was focussed solely on a particularly hypnotic girl who seemed too beautiful to be Human, and a large patch of dense mist that the others gave a wide berth. Peering closely into the fog, Galen thought he could discern a pair of eyes. He became certain of it when one of them winked at him.

"He looks like he's never seen a ghost before," the fog remarked, thickening until Galen could make out four distinct figures, all of them laughing at him.

He drew himself up. "Well, I haven't. I grew up on a Human planet and I was too young to fight in the war. There's lots of kids like me back home who have never met a Titan before. I figure if we're all going to be neighbours for a few years, I better get used to it, and quick."

Somehow, his matter-of-fact statement managed to kill all conversation in the aircar as it sped through the Colony to what Galen recognised from his initial briefing as the Nyx

Dome.

So he had been given his first choice, then. The cold dome where no Mer could swim, so he'd be safe from them. Maybe it was childish, but Galen didn't care. Being able to sleep safely at night without fear of attack meant a lot to him. After all, he still had occasional nightmares about waking up alone in his cabin on the *Poseidon*, his headphones in his ears, the music drowned out by the emergency sirens blaring the ship's death knell. He'd stumbled onto the lifeboat with nothing but the music player, and the hope that his parents would be waiting for him when he was rescued. A forlorn hope, for sure. He'd been the only survivor from the *Poseidon*, and to this day, he still didn't know why. Had Halcyon chosen not to kill him, because he was a child, while slaughtering everyone else? If so, she'd made a huge mistake that day. That child was now a man, and one who wouldn't let anything stand between him and vengeance for his parents' murder.

The aircar announced his apartment number.

Galen unclenched his fists and stepped out of the aircar. It zoomed away, leaving him alone in the corridor outside his door. Outside what would be home for the next five years.

Galen took a deep breath, palmed open the door, and stepped inside.

Only to discover the apartment was already occupied.

"…I repeat, restrict temperatures within all living spaces to a lower limit of two…no, make it five degrees above the freezing point of water. Anyone who wants lower temperatures than that will have to apply to Maintenance and only if appropriate insulation is fitted to all the apartment's pipework will it be allowed," the woman said. A floor-cleaning robot hummed around her feet, siphoning water off the floor.

An electronic voice protested, "You do not have authorisation to impose controls on all living spaces, or this one. Resident number – "

"Space that!" the woman snapped. "My authorisation is ALI-407102 Maintenance override. Stick that up your circuits and do as you're told."

Galen liked her already.

"Processing," the recorded voice replied. "Authorisation confirmed. Any further orders?"

"Give me a damage report. How many apartments are affected by the burst pipes?"

A pause, then the electronic voice said, "Just those on this side of the inner ring of this level. No other apartments had sub-zero temperatures for an extended period."

The woman sighed, her shoulders relaxing along with her voice. "Good. I want temperatures matched to those in 407 until the ice has melted in all affected apartments, and I want floor cleaning robots activated in all of them. Get me every Maintenance worker we have in the Colony, and a load of replacement pipes. This is urgent."

"Implementing orders now," the voice said.

As if on command, the communications device on Galen's wrist sounded an alert.

The woman whirled around, so her surprised eyes met his. She wasn't more than a girl, really, despite her authoritative orders to the building management AI. Yet her dark eyes seemed to x-ray his soul, if he believed in such a thing.

Galen tried to shake off the effect of her hypnotic stare. Did that make her a Titan like the Watch at the entrance? "How many apartments have burst pipes?"

Her eyes widened for a moment. "Enough to keep me busy all day. Some idiot set these rooms to temperatures below freezing, without realising that some other idiot had forgotten to insulate the water pipes against freezing. Probably someone who'd never seen snow before, or what ice can do to pipes. My money's on a stupid ship-born Titan." Her brows drew so low they nearly met over the bridge of her nose.

Hating Titans made her Human, then. Just a

really pretty one. Galen blew out a breath he hadn't known he was holding. Human and his type and here. Whoever she was, he wanted her.

"Aren't we supposed to be trying to get along?" Galen said. "You know, us and the Titans, now the war's over?"

The girl snorted. "Oh, sure. The war's over and we live under a peace treaty, so we're not supposed to kill each other, but there was nothing in the treaty about banning stupidity. So I guess we'll just have to live with that."

Galen laughed. She wasn't stupid, that was for sure. "I'm Galen," he said, extending a hand in greeting. "I'm supposed to be the environmental engineer responsible for the Colony, and while I don't think I've officially started work yet, I think your AI just conscripted me." He pointed at his comm. "I've changed a few pipes in my time. I did my apprenticeship on shipboard environmental systems. Nothing as state of the art as this place. Our ship was falling apart, cobbled together from spare parts and scrap metal in the first place. You'd replace one thing, only to find something else had fallen off while you were working. I can handle pipe replacements."

Her cool fingers meshed with his as she shook his hand. Her eyes lit up. "So you're the genius engineer Ira told me about. I thought you'd be older." Her mischievous grin did things to Galen's insides.

"I'm twenty-four, and I've been working as an engineer for a decade. Plenty old enough to know what I'm doing," Galen snapped to hide the tumult inside. She couldn't be any older than he was. In fact, she looked younger. And she was a Maintenance worker, which made her his subordinate. "How many apartments need replacement pipes?" he repeated.

The girl lifted her eyes to the ceiling. "Answer him."

"Fifty-two, not including the two already repaired," the electronic voice said.

"Twenty-six each, then," the girl said. She

flashed another impish grin. "How fast can you fix pipes, genius? Want to wager something on it? Loser has to make the winner dinner."

How had she known he'd wanted to ask her to dinner? Galen shook his head. She hadn't. "You're on. One condition, though."

She raised her eyebrows, waving for him to continue.

"Tell me your name."

She let out a peal of laughter. "Sure thing, Galen. I'm Allie, and it's good to have you on board. Genius or not, anyone who can fix pipes is a good man in my book." Allie winked. "I'll go left, and you go right. I already fixed the pipes in your next door neighbours' place. A wolverine shifter family. Good thing the ventilation's still working well."

Galen watched her head down the corridor, unable to take his eyes off her.

Allie glanced over her shoulder. "Staring at my arse won't win you your wager, genius. Nor will it get you any closer to getting your hands on it."

Feeling his face grow hot, Galen turned away, but not before he heard her laughter ring out down the corridor. He had to win this wager, he swore. His reputation depended on it.

And maybe more besides, he thought, envisioning what she looked like without her standard-issue coverall. One day he wanted to find out how well fantasy matched the reality.

FIVE

Allie hummed as she connected her final replacement pipe. She'd encountered a few new colonists during her repairs, but this apartment's occupants, like the people who'd move into the others in this ring, were probably still queueing up in the cargo bay. She told the AI to make the temperatures comfortably cool in the apartments she'd worked on. Now the ice was melted and cleaned away, no one would ever know about the damage to their new homes.

Well, except Galen and Ira. And that shifter family who'd reported the ice in the first place.

"How many pipes does Galen have left to fix, Col?" Allie asked, unable to resist.

"Three," the AI replied. "I do not understand your need for pet names."

"Col," Allie repeated, spelling the word out. "Short for the Colony. It's what I'll call you. It feels too impersonal just shouting at the walls without a name. Now you have a name, I can pretend you're another very helpful person in the next room."

"Illogical sentiment," the AI said.

Allie laughed merrily. "Yep. That's why you're an AI and I'm not. Don't ever change, Col. Now, how long do you think it'll take Galen to finish work? I don't want to embarrass him by showing up early. The poor boy is supposed to be my superior. He should at least feel like it on occasion."

"Forty-three minutes."

Allie whistled. "That long? I wish I'd

brought a book." She thought for a moment. "Can you bring up footage of the arrivals area on the main screen in here? The occupants of this apartment won't be here for an hour or so, right?"

"The shuttle carrying the sasquatches has not yet landed," the AI said. "The apartment will be vacant for an estimated six hours and twenty-six minutes."

"Mine for the moment, then," Allie said, sanitising her hands before pulling out a ration bar. "Arrivals area, on screen."

She sank down on the floor to watch the colonists oohing and aahing over their first glimpse of the Colony interior as they entered Metropolis. Titan and Human alike looked just as awestruck. Maybe Ira was right and their two peoples weren't as dissimilar as they appeared. That's why this huge social experiment had to work. Allie would do everything in her power to help it along. She craved peace more than even chocolate. Peace meant no more loved ones would die, and maybe, just maybe, she could let her crushed heart love again after so many losses.

Even if there was no one left in the system for her, at least she'd have the satisfaction of knowing others could find love, and keep it. Take young Galen, for example. It was only a matter of time before he found the right girl and persuaded her to share his quarters. Then the two of them would work on repopulation like rabbits, the hopping creatures she'd seen someone unloading into the agricultural dome.

Lucky boy, to have such a future. Allie had no children, but now she had no partner to give them to her, so they seemed like even more of a tantalising dream than ever before. Never mind. There were plenty of children pouring into the Colony down below, she saw on her screen. Children who would be guaranteed employment as ambassadors when they left the Colony and reached adulthood. Quite the coup for their parents. Who wouldn't jump at the chance to secure their children's future with an opportunity like this?

Allie saw so much hope in the Colony. Perhaps Titans and Humans truly could achieve peace in a place like this. And if they could do it here, they could do it anywhere. What price wouldn't she pay for peace, above and beyond the one she'd paid already?

Allie wiped away a stray tear. There was no point crying over the past. She'd mourned long enough before the war ended. Now it was time to look to the future, and find out how Galen was going with his pipes.

"What's the ETA on Galen getting back to his apartment, Col?" Allie asked.

"Minus four minutes. He appears to be smug."

Allie rose. "Get a robot to clean up the crumbs, please, Col." She left the apartment, striding along the corridor back to where Galen waited. The man did look smug, but his smirk widened into a genuine grin when he spotted her.

"Looks like I beat you," he said cheerfully. "But my mother would never forgive me if I let a lady take me to dinner, especially on a first date. Shall we?" He waved open his door and gestured for her to go inside.

Allie couldn't help laughing. She hadn't heard gallantry like this in a very long time.

Galen's refrigerator turned out to contain very different rations to her limited kitchen. While she'd been given a week's worth of ration bars to sustain her until the shops and eateries opened in Metropolis, he had frozen meals that could be reheated into something that actually resembled Human food. His apartment didn't have a view of the stars, and it was a lot smaller than hers, but there was space for a sofa and a tiny retractable table with two chairs where they sat to eat their meal.

After two mouthfuls of her shrimp pasta, Allie heartily regretted requesting ration bars for the week. Galen's food actually tasted good. She might have to spend some of her credits in the restaurants after all. She hoped they opened soon. Maybe Galen would be willing to join her for dinner on occasion. The young engineer wasn't bad company at all.

SIX

Galen couldn't remember ever talking so much in his life, yet Allie drank in every word while her honey-coloured eyes seemed to beg for more. Several times he had to tell himself he was imagining it. No woman had ever listened to him like this – not even his mother, and she'd loved him.

Still the words spilled out. He told her about how he was orphaned at fourteen, but because he was already an apprentice engineer he'd been allowed to continue his studies at the engineering college, finishing his degree at eighteen. How the other graduates all went to war and didn't come back, while he was given a job in the terraforming lab, working on prototypes and new techniques that he inevitably found ways to improve. Then, when the war ended, he'd signed up for the Colony, after discovering that a lot of his inventions were being put to use in the domes. So while he hadn't designed the place, he knew all the technology intimately.

Take their water supply, for instance. Unlike Styx, the water planet that relied mostly on desalination for its drinking water supply, where he'd first been apprenticed, New Hope had a ready-made water supply from the reservoirs beneath the surface, which is why they'd built the Colony on this very spot. Powerful freshwater springs bubbled up from the ground here, providing the entire population with more water than they'd ever need. Of course, they still recycled all their water within the Colony, to keep their pollutants from damaging the environment outside, but the treated wastewater was only used for irrigation, unlike on the colony ships, where they'd had to use it for everything.

At that point, Galen's mind caught up with his mouth. "I'm sorry. I'm boring you. What possessed me to talk about plumbing to possibly the most beautiful woman I've ever met…" He turned red.

Allie laughed softly and shook her head. "We've both spent half the day working on plumbing. Believe me, it's not boring at all, especially if it'll make my job easier. Now I know why they said you're a genius. You practically designed all the systems we use in the Colony. If I have trouble with anything, you know you're the first person I'll call."

"Any time," he replied eagerly. "And not just for work, either. Anything you need. Just call and I'll be there." He'd barely known the woman a day and here he was, offering to do anything for her. But it felt right, somehow.

"What about if I want someone to join me for dinner, so I don't have to eat alone?"

Warm, honey eyes drew him inexorably in. Galen swallowed. Oh, he wanted in, all right. "Especially then."

She dropped her gaze to the floor, as if what she saw in his eyes was too intense. "I'll remember. But on that note, I should probably go. I have no doubt half the Colony will have pressing maintenance issues tomorrow and we'll both need all the rest we can get. Thank you for a lovely evening, Galen. It's the best time I've had since…well, a while, anyway."

She rose swiftly and was out the door before Galen could move. So much for a good night kiss.

"Good night," he called as the door slid shut behind her.

He disposed of the remains of dinner, then leaned against the counter. Allie was right – it had been a lovely evening, one of the best he'd had in a while. He'd never hit it off so well with a woman before. What a time to find someone so wonderful, though. Couldn't fate have waited until he'd found and dealt with Halcyon before it rewarded him with an introduction to Allie?

His blood ran cold. What if Halcyon managed to attack the Colony before he found her…and Allie got hurt? He'd lost enough already. While she wasn't his yet, he still didn't want to lose the chance that one day she might be. He wouldn't give Halcyon the opportunity to hurt her. No, he'd strike first, however he could, Galen resolved.

Starting tomorrow, he'd hunt down the homicidal siren and end her. Then he'd be free to pursue happiness with Allie, knowing they'd be safe.

The siren's days were numbered.

SEVEN

Allie had just dismissed her skimmer when she heard a woman calling her name. She turned to find Violet climbing out of an aircar, holding a bottle aloft in each hand.

"We finally got everyone into the Colony, so it's time to celebrate!" Violet announced.

Allie eyed the bottles. "What are those?"

"Finest fey moonshine. One of the Humans confiscated it from a kitsune who was trying to smuggle them in. I said I'd dispose of them properly, and so here I am!" Violet beamed. "Do you think we can drink them both tonight?"

"Not if I have to work in the morning," Allie replied, palming open her door and ushering Violet inside. "I've spent all day fixing plumbing in the Nyx Dome. The universe only knows what I'll have to deal with tomorrow."

Violet tossed her dark hair. "Well, a Human engineer, for starters. One who's afraid of Titans. He kept touching his implant, like it was some sort of magical amulet that could protect him from me." She snorted. "He might have been better off with an amulet. Those implants don't do anything except mark him as gullible. Maybe that was his name – Gill, Gull, something like that."

"Galen?" It couldn't be. He hadn't seemed afraid of her at all, and they'd spent most of the evening together. In fact, she'd thought he was working up the courage to kiss her right there at the end, which is why she'd made her excuses and left. She'd loved and lost once.

Allie didn't think she could survive having her heart ripped out like that again.

"I think that was his name. Hard to remember. There were so many of them today. Young guy with a thing for music." Violet set the bottles on the bench. "Do you have any glasses?"

"Col, where are the glasses?" Allie asked.

A wall panel popped open.

"Thanks, Col."

Violet stared at Allie. "We have an AI controlling this facility? I don't remember that in the briefing documents."

"Of course. I'm probably not supposed to ask it to open cupboards and things, but who do you think responds when you ask for the temperature to be turned down in your apartment?" Allie asked, setting two glasses beside the bottle.

Violet peered around. "I use the controls. I don't talk to the walls. Is it…watching us?"

Allie laughed softly. "Col, are there cameras in the apartments?"

"There is no surveillance in private quarters," the AI said.

Allie shrugged. "Guess not, then. Why, were you thinking of doing something naughty you don't want anyone to see?"

Violet smiled. "Maybe. But Watch officers are supposed to be so good all the time, keeping the peace and all. Did they make you sit through an hour-long briefing on the importance of peace?"

She'd had to sit through months of peace talks as Humans and Titans gradually decided not to kill each other. Surely that was enough for anyone. Allie shook her head. "No, I must have missed that briefing. Fixing pipes today, or something."

Violet rolled her eyes. "Lucky you. Just thinking about it makes me need a drink." She uncorked a bottle and poured an inch of viscous purple liquid into each glass. "Is it supposed to look like that?" She lifted the glasses, eyeing the milky, mauve contents with suspicion.

Allie seized a glass. "I don't know. I've never been able to afford fey moonshine. To peace." She took a careful sip.

Violet gulped hers, then choked. "Stars, it's fey rocket fuel. That's potent!"

"Mm, it's strong, but I like it," Allie said, savouring her second sip. "I taste flowers, kisses and seafoam." And memories, she thought but didn't say.

"I think I just coughed up a lung," Violet said. "Is there any chance of some chocolate?"

Allie set her glass down. "Of course! How could I forget?" She retrieved a block from the refrigerator and passed it to Violet. "Have as much as you like. I think I'll finish my drink first."

"You can have all of it. Both bottles," Violet said darkly.

"Really? Then you should keep the block of chocolate. Fair trade." Allie reached for another block and unwrapped it. "We'll share this one."

They both ate in silence for a moment,

savouring the sweetness of what Allie knew was the best chocolate in the system.

Then Violet started to laugh. "You know," she said, "I had you pegged as trying to seduce me down by the blast doors. I expected you to ask me for a favour, something I'm not supposed to give you. I figured if I brought you some liquor, maybe it would mellow you a little and you'd go easy on me. You're nothing like I expected."

Allie regarded her. "What did you expect?"

Violet's laughter died. "Colder. Harder. Not…chocolate." Fear darkened her eyes.

Allie hummed, hoping to set the succubus more at her ease. "I am here to pursue peace, Violet. I've had my fill of war. Now, why don't you tell me about your day downstairs? I'd love to hear your impressions of our new colonists."

Violet nodded and opened her mouth to recount the first of what would be many reports.

EIGHT

"It has to be here," Galen said to himself as he palmed open the hatch to Maintenance Storeroom 6. If anyone asked, he was taking inventory of their spare parts and tools, but no one had. After all, he was the boss. Who would question him, as long as his Maintenance crews were out in the Colony, dealing with all the teething troubles that plagued such a high-tech new facility? No one, that's who.

He had plenty to show for his time in the

previous five storerooms. All sorts of equipment that was supposed to be present simply wasn't, or the numbers were lower than expected. He'd called Allie, the most promising of his staff, to ask whether the missing equipment had already been used in repairs but not documented, and she'd laughed merrily.

"Boss, you're underestimating how lazy Maintenance staff are. Going to the storerooms and picking up our own equipment? Hardly. We message the AI, and have it sent. If there's an inventory issue, then it's Col forgetting things, or that equipment never arrived. Who's more likely to make a mistake — the AI, or the people who stocked this place?"

Galen had to admit he trusted the machine more than people, though he had to shake his head at Allie's name for the AI. Machines didn't need names. He'd thanked her and ended the call.

Sighing, he counted the pumps again. Four hundred and seventy-three, when there were only supposed to be four hundred and seventy-two. Skimping on supplies was one thing, but adding to them? Not likely. One of the pumps had to be his package.

But which one?

Galen scanned the shelves. They wouldn't have made it too obvious, but surely they'd left him some clue as to which one held more than just a standard-issue water pump.

There.

One of the boxes at the back bulged slightly at the top, as though someone hadn't closed it properly. Galen shifted the other boxes out the way until he could reach the suspicious one. The moment he lifted it up, he knew he had the right one. It weighed much more than the others.

He wanted to open it right away, but this was hardly the place for it. His office, or the workshop adjacent to it, would be the perfect place. After all, even if the surveillance cameras recorded everything, it wouldn't look suspicious for an engineer to be modifying or building equipment in the dedicated workshop designed for that purpose.

Reluctantly, Galen finished his stocktake before lugging the box back to his office. He was relieved to be able to drop his burden on his desk as soon as the door slid shut behind him. Whatever was in the box sure was heavy.

He flipped the lid open and found a sheaf of papers. Pages of schematics about the water supply pipework to the domes, as well as the design for a destructive device that matched those Halcyon was known to use.

It wasn't common knowledge, but the siren terrorist had detonated nuclear fission bombs at several of the sites where she'd left no survivors. It's how she'd destroyed the *Poseidon*, too, though the ship was too deep below the surface by the time the bomb went off for it to have done much damage.

It was both an insult and a promise to the Humans she loved to slaughter. Humans had destroyed their own world through nuclear weapons, she seemed to say, so she'd finish the job and drive their species to extinction with their own technology.

Galen swallowed. He didn't need to open the wooden box inside the cardboard one to know what it held. Fissile material. Some sort of radioisotope. Uranium, he imagined. Enough to build a nuclear weapon and destroy the entire Colony.

He'd known when he joined forces with the shadowy Humans First movement that they hated Titans with a passion Galen would never understand. Not just those who fought and killed like Halcyon, but all Titans. Some of their zealots believed the peace effort was merely a smokescreen while the Titans bided their time, waiting to strike and wipe out Humans for good.

So they'd given him the material to make a pre-emptive strike that would send peace up in a mushroom cloud of smoke, leaving New Hope to its native denizens.

Galen took a deep breath and opened the wooden box. Inside the lead-lined compartments he found four solid metal canisters, each containing a metal rod tarnished to a dull grey so they looked like cast iron or weathered steel. Ordinary metals, instead of stuff that could blow them all sky-high with the right detonator.

Galen was no terrorist. He hated Halcyon, sure, but that was personal. He had no intention of building a nuclear bomb. Instead, he'd build something that looked like one, but only put in half the uranium so there'd only be an ordinary explosion, with some radiation contamination. Not enough to kill anyone outside the immediate area, but enough to make it look like Halcyon had tried to sabotage the Colony.

The Watch would have to investigate, and Halcyon herself probably would, too, knowing she hadn't set the bomb. Either way, the siren would surface and Galen would get his chance.

He'd have to make sure the bomb was away from all the living quarters, and detonate it at night when the force screens were down, to make sure as few people were nearby as possible. He didn't want to hurt anyone. It had to look like an accident, going off prematurely with too little fuel. Galen was confident he could do that.

After all, Allie had called him a genius, hadn't she? Time to see if he could finally outsmart the siren.

NINE

By the end of her first fortnight, Allie found herself humming all the time, she was so happy. Galen had assigned her the task of all the eating house fitouts in Metropolis and she couldn't wait until they were all open. While she finalised the plumbing in each premises, she got to see the menus and sometimes even sample the dishes they planned to offer their customers. By the time she'd finished her job in one restaurant or bar, the new owners had caught her contagious good mood, and after signing off on the job, they inevitably offered her a free meal once they opened.

Soon, she had enough invitations to keep her from cooking for the next month. And all the flavours…Human foods even more diverse than Titan ones, as if they'd compensated for all looking so similar to one another by varying their cooking styles as widely as they dared, while still ensuring the product was edible. Eateries that sold only ice cream or chocolate or coffee or tacos or sushi or crepes or…what in the world was a kebab? Allie wasn't certain, but she definitely intended to find out.

Maybe it was just her imagination, but there seemed to be more Human establishments than Titan ones. Or perhaps all the happy Humans were recommending her services to their friends, so she was kept too busy to visit more than the occasional Titan bar or two. Allie didn't mind. The more people she met, the more she learned about what had brought them to the Colony in the first place.

Some had come for the money, or the security it offered them and their children. Some came for the promise of peace, at least for a little while. But they spoke of peace as a dream, a temporary ideal that none of them thought would last.

Allie understood. If she hadn't lost her husband in the war, maybe her thoughts would be more focussed on mundane concerns.

"Are you finished already?" Melete, the muse who owned the exotic dance club, asked. "You'll have to come back when we open. I have dancers to appeal to everyone. When they hear you're the one who installed the showers that will be the envy of every dance club in Metropolis, they'll all be clamouring to thank you. Human, Titan, male, female, more than one…where ever your tastes lie, we can satisfy you, I'm sure."

"Thank you. I'll keep that in mind if I find myself lonely one evening. But you really don't owe me anything. I try to be as quick as I can. I have…many demands on my time," Allie said carefully. As if to illustrate her point, her comm sounded an alert. "Speak of the devil…"

Melete nodded respectfully and retreated deeper into the club.

At times like these, Allie appreciated the effect her reputation had on people. On Titans, anyway. She had yet to meet a Human who'd heard of her in relation to anything except her wizardry with plumbing.

Allie answered the call with a cheerful, "Hi, this is Allie."

"I thought you were still working, not spending time in a strip club." Ira, the Titan in charge of the Watch on New Hope, didn't sound impressed.

"You're just jealous your job doesn't let you spend much time here," Allie said lightly, not fooled by his tone. She'd known him for long enough to know he was nowhere near as stern as he seemed. "Plumbing is very important in the washrooms of a dance club. But the showers are all installed now, with lovely water pressure, if I do say so myself. So, what can I do for you? You got a leaky pipe in your office?"

"More like one that's blocked. You haven't reported for two weeks. Time to come in."

"Yes, sir. I'll get that pipe unblocked directly," Allie said, snapping off a salute.

"Not now. After dinner. Just make sure it's tonight." Ira ended the call abruptly. He was a busy man who didn't have time for goodbyes.

Maybe he should spend more time in strip clubs, or at least doing whatever he called fun, Allie mused, breathing in the scents of the eateries that were open for business. A particularly rich, salty smell caught her attention more than the others. Making a sound that came out very close to a moan, Allie caught herself, closed her mouth, and followed the smell to its source. A shop that sold something called pizza, apparently. More new Human food she hadn't tried.

Food worth sharing. On a whim, she called Galen.

After a few seconds, he answered, "Hello?" He sounded distracted.

"What are you doing for dinner?" she asked.

"I don't know. That's hours away," he said.

He must have been working as hard as she had today. "Nope. It's now. Tonight is pizza night, if you get your bossy butt down to Metropolis in the next ten minutes. Sending you my location." She sent her coordinates to Galen, then held her breath as she waited for his response.

"My bossy butt?"

"You're the boss, and you have a butt. Bossy butt. Don't you like pizza? It smells incredible." She breathed deeply. If he took more than ten minutes, she was going in without him.

"Pizza sounds great. I'll get down there as fast as I can. Bye."

She didn't have to wait long. Galen stepped off a skimmer, looking like he'd been hard at work in the workshop all day. Allie probably didn't look much better, but it wasn't like they were on a date or anything.

"You look beautiful," he breathed, his admiring eyes reinforcing the compliment.

Allie laughed. "You're just saying that because I had to deal with all the burst pipes today, while you got to stay in the office. One of the perks of being the boss, boss."

Galen just shook his head and raised his eyes to the sign above the pizza shop. "So this is where you want to eat?"

"Sure do." Allie led the way inside. The rich aroma intensified, reminding her that the ration bars she'd eaten for lunch were a long time gone.

"I smell why," Galen said, inhaling deeply. "I haven't had pizza since my mother…"

"Is she a good cook, your mother?" Allie asked. She didn't dare mention hers. Her own mother had never cooked a thing in her life.

"She was." Galen closed his eyes. "She died when I was fourteen."

A decade ago. Roughly the same time as Allie had lost her husband. "I'm sorry," she said sincerely.

Galen sighed. "Me, too. But not as sorry as the one who killed her will be. They told me she was a casualty of war, but I know better."

Allie's sympathy overflowed. "Your mother wasn't a soldier?"

Galen shook his head. "A scientist. I get my skills with machines from her. She encouraged me to tinker when I was a kid, letting me build things in her workshop. My father wanted me to be a doctor, but I wasn't interested in how Human bodies work as much as machines. I think I disappointed him, but he died when I was a kid, too, so I'll never know what either of them think about what I've become."

"I'm sure they'd be proud of all you've achieved. You're very young to hold the position you do here in the Colony," Allie said. Her parents had made no secret of their disapproval for her choices, but then she'd never really been close to them.

"If there's some sort of afterlife for them, I hope they will be," Galen replied. He waved at the menu board. "What do you want for dinner?"

Allie chose one pizza, Galen chose another, and they both sat at a corner table to wait for their order.

"So what about you? Where did you grow up?" Galen asked.

Allie choked on her drink. If he didn't know, then she couldn't tell him. "We moved around a lot, so no one place really stands out. These five years on New Hope will probably be the longest I've ever lived in one place."

Galen nodded. "We moved around a lot, too, when I lived with my parents. Dad was the ship's doctor, and Mum was one of the technicians, so we went from ship to ship until they died."

Anxious to keep the conversation on his family and not hers, Allie ventured, "How did they die? You never did say."

"They were on the *Poseidon* when it was attacked. They didn't make it to the lifeboats in time." Galen plucked the straw out of his cup, threw it on the table and drank from the lip of his cup instead.

"Why weren't you with them?" Allie asked.

Galen laughed. "I was. I was in the cabin we shared, while they both worked the evening shift. When I heard the alarms, I headed for the lifeboats, but I was the only one. There were no other survivors."

The image of a sole lifeboat, floating alone in the waves, popped into Allie's head. Orphaned at fourteen and then alone at sea for so long before he was rescued. "It must have been terrible for you," she whispered.

Galen slammed his cup down on the table. "It's just part of war, or at least that's what everyone told me. The innocent suffer, while killers go free. That's why this war had to end, and this place has to succeed. No more killing."

Allie felt the peculiar urge to kiss him. "Absolutely. No more killing." She raised her drink in a toast that Galen seconded.

Their pizzas appeared, and Allie waited just

long enough to watch Galen take his first bite before she tried to emulate him. It was messy and unfamiliar, but by the stars, it tasted so good she didn't care.

"Oh!" she mumbled around a slice. "We have to come back here."

Galen grinned. "Next week? I spotted a couple of places I'd like to try, too. One that sold yiros, which I haven't had in forever."

"Yiros?" Allie hadn't heard of that one.

"Ah, seasoned meat and sauce and salad, all wrapped up in flatbread? Some people call them kebabs," Galen explained, gesturing with his hands.

The mysterious kebabs. "Tomorrow, then, if they're open?" Allie suggested.

Galen swallowed. "A third date already, and a fourth next week? Careful, you'll have all the Maintenance guys talking. They'll think you like me."

Let them talk. People always did. Especially about her. "I do like you. I'll have dinner with you every night until we've tried every restaurant in Metropolis. And the other guys can talk until they lose their voices or find something more interesting to discuss."

Galen's eyes warmed. "I'd like that."

"What, them not talking about us? I'll see what I can do." Allie resolved to take care of that problem tomorrow. The Titans would be easy. The Humans might take a bit more effort. Only a little, though.

Galen shook his head. "Gossip can't be stopped. It's like radiation – once it's been released, there's no stopping it. That's why we left Earth."

"Sure there is. It just takes time and patience. Thousands of years, in some cases, like Earth. And there are ways to stop it. Radiation shielding, for one. Every problem has a solution. It just comes at a cost. Sometimes a higher cost than we can afford, or are willing to pay." Allie bit into a slice of pizza, forcing herself to concentrate on the flavour and nothing else. She already knew there was no price too high for peace, at least from her perspective. She'd given everything she had, and she'd give more still.

"Even peace," Galen said, like he was reading her mind. "Peace is worth any price."

More than ever, Allie wanted to kiss him. But she couldn't do any such thing. She had a meeting with Ira tonight, and she didn't want to start anything with Galen that she couldn't finish. Another night, perhaps.

TEN

When dinner ended, Galen debated whether to ask Allie back to his apartment, or just kiss her goodnight and leave the invitation for another night. It was too soon, he decided, as she made no move to get close enough to him for a kiss. Instead, she waved as she stepped onto a skimmer to take her home.

Galen was tempted to step onto the hovering platform behind her, wrapping his arms around her body so they could go back to her place or his and get closer still.

He shook his head. Not until he knew she was safe. Safe from the clutches of the siren. Until then, he'd have to content himself with explicit dreams about her. And finish his project sooner.

Instead of taking his own skimmer home, he headed back to the workshop. If he finished it tonight, he could set the bomb in place before the end of the week, let it do its damage, and hunt the siren before next week's pizza date with Allie. He'd have to buy some alcohol to celebrate. Then, he'd tell her everything about his successful hunt for his parents' killer, so she could celebrate the victory with him. War would never be over for terrorists like Halcyon. The siren wasn't reasonable the way people like him and Allie were. The siren was a crazed killer who had to be stopped before she killed again.

And he was the man to do it, he was certain of it. What had Allie said tonight? What price was he willing to pay for peace?

"Almost anything, except her life," Galen swore. He wouldn't let the siren take anyone else he cared about. Never again.

ELEVEN

"So what do you have to report?" Ira's ice-blue eyes regarded Allie across the desk.

She knew he expected her to sit in the client's chair across from him, but she was feeling playful this evening, so she perched on the edge of the desk instead. "Aside from the expected complaints about shoddy work done by some of the other construction people that's caused me two weeks' worth of grief with no end in sight, nothing." Allie smiled.

"Your Colony is so full of happy people it even makes me cheerful. I spend so much of my day singing as I go from apartment to apartment, or business to business, fixing things. upgrading things. You know. All the things a girl has to do to keep the water running around here."

"There have been six fights and five brawls today alone in the common areas of the Colony. That's not a sign of happy people."

Allie shrugged. "It could be. I've met men who were happiest when they were punching or hurting someone. And there are those who enjoy the pain. It takes all sorts to make a universe." She paused, puzzled. "What do you mean, six fights and five brawls? What's the difference? Aren't they the same thing?"

Ira tapped his tablet and held it out as video footage appeared on the screen. "In this fight, a pair of shifters attacked a Human." While Allie watched the brutal attack in horror, Ira continued, "A kitsune was badly beaten by what she says was a Human, but she wasn't sure. A Human and an incubus got into a punch-up over a succubus outside the strip club you invited me to this evening. In the Arbor Dome this afternoon, six Humans attacked a giant. Some shifters rushed to his aid, and then some more Humans, until some fifty people, both Human and Titan, were arrested and fined for brawling in public. We're not sure what started the other brawls — sometimes the surveillance cameras don't capture everything. All we do know is the one place brawls don't happen is the Aqua Dome. And wherever you happen to be."

Allie wet her lips. "How many of your Watch have noticed that?"

"I'm pretty sure all of them noticed the Aqua Dome is peaceful. It might take them a lot longer to associate you with the unusual patches of peace, if all this unpeaceful activity keeps them busy."

Allie breathed out a sigh of relief. "I can't be everywhere at once. And I'm not doing much, honest. Just…calming things. Putting people in a good mood. There's nothing wrong with that."

"There are quite a few who'd argue that doing anything to control their thinking is wrong," Ira said.

"Only if they're aware of it," Allie argued. "They don't complain when they're being brainwashed by bigots, or warmongers, or advertising, or the smell of a new restaurant wafting down the street, enticing them inside. Having a humming plumber in their house is no different to any of those things!"

"They can reject ideas, or advertising, or even food, but they can't resist you," Ira said.

"Aww, that's so sweet of you to say. Does that mean you can't resist me, either?" Allie fluttered her eyelashes and slid off the desk. She laughed, knowing Ira was one of the few Titans she'd met who could. Maybe that's why she liked him so much. It couldn't be his sense of humour. "I'm not asking them to do anything outside their nature. I'm not controlling them. I'm simply…calming things.

Bringing a little more peace into this place. Like we agreed we wanted."

"I want you to find the troublemakers. I know there are some in here. One of the most militant anti-peace movements, the Humans First group, boasted that the Colony wouldn't last six months before someone blew it up. They have sympathisers inside the Colony, I'm certain of it. Find them before anyone gets hurt. Your supervisor has connections to them. What about him?"

"My supervisor? You mean Galen?" Allie couldn't help laughing. "He's the last man I'd consider if I was looking for a terrorist. His passion for peace is only slightly less fervent than my own. There's absolutely no way he could be planning on blowing this place up. Next thing you know, you'll be trying to convince me that he's building a bomb."

Ira looked annoyed. "He could be. He has the technical knowledge and the tools to construct one."

Allie shrugged. "So do I, but you don't see

me doing it." She held up her hands in surrender. "All right, all right. While I'm working to keep the water running, I'll keep an eye out for terrorists. And I'll ask Galen if he recognises anyone he used to know from the Humans First group. In between singing."

Before Ira could ask her to do anything else, she left, humming. Galen building a bomb. Honestly. Maybe Ira had a sense of humour after all.

TWELVE

Galen finished taping the explosives to the inside the pump casing and breathed a sigh of relief. It was only half-full, even with the detonator in place – plenty of space for the radioactive payload, and yet still small enough to fit in his tool bag. If he wanted to destroy the city, all he had to do was put all the uranium rods into the casing beside the explosives and when the whole thing detonated…the city would be nothing but a radioactive crater. Not a single soul among those locked in the Colony would survive. It was a sobering thought.

If he'd known nuclear weapons could be so small, he wouldn't have been so surprised Humans had blown up their own planet with them. In fact, he was stunned that they'd lasted as long as they had. But he had to put this somewhere a siren would place it, not a Human, to make it look like it was Halcyon's work. That meant underwater. He knew just the spot, too – where the water supply bubbled up under the Aqua Dome from the springs deep below New Hope's surface. Without a set of Mer gills and a tail, he'd have to use a rebreather mask and fins, but he'd found plenty of those in Storeroom Five during his stocktake.

Someone tapped him on the shoulder.

Galen pulled off his headphones. "What?"

"How's the new satellite doing?" Alpen asked.

Galen stared at the grey-skinned incubus.

"It's not a satellite."

Alpen shrugged. "We've all been placing bets on what you're building. One of the other guys thinks it's some sort of anti-surveillance device, so we can have strippers in the workshop without the Watch knowing. Another one said it's a still for brewing alcohol. I figured it was a communications satellite so you could sell black market communications to the rest of the system. Guess I was wrong. Unless you're lying so you can keep all the call fees for yourself. You'd be rich by the time you got out of here."

"It's not a satellite," Galen repeated, turning off his music player. "It's a water purifier. Some of the residents in the Aqua Dome have reported contaminants in the water, so I'll be putting this in the pipes below the dome to see if it can fix things, or at least remove enough contaminants to stop the complaints." That was the cover story he'd thought up and he was sticking to it.

"What sort of contaminants?" Alpen asked.

"I remember one of the ships I was working on had this hideous stench to the water supply…"

"Don't know," Galen interrupted. "Can't detect anything out of the ordinary, but the Mer insist there's a problem. This is me trying to fix it." He waved his hand over the pump casing.

Alpen shrugged. "Good luck. Unless you need anything, I'm done for the day. Heading home for a meal. If the HVAC system has any hiccups you can't handle, comm me."

"It'll be fine. See you tomorrow." Galen watched him go, then donned his headphones and switched the music back on.

Allie had suggested they go to a fairy bar tonight, but she'd called to cancel an hour ago, saying she'd gotten caught up in a repair job over in one of the residential domes, so they'd have to reschedule for tomorrow instead.

Knowing he'd almost finished the bomb, Galen had decided to bring the schedule forward and put it in place tonight, so he could celebrate with Allie properly tomorrow. He'd decided not to detonate it for a few days. Maybe he'd even set it off tomorrow, while he was on that date with Allie. He'd have a solid alibi then. Not that he should need one, but you could never be too careful.

He'd originally planned to plant the bomb late at night, when no one was around, but he'd since realised that would look far too suspicious. Instead, he carried the modified pump in one box and the uranium rods inside his toolbox, looking for all the world like a plumber about to go replace a pump. Routine maintenance.

Sure enough, no one in the packed aircar gave him a second glance. They glared at his burdens as he squeezed in, before shuffling aside without a word. It was a long aircar ride to the base of the Aqua Dome, but by the time he reached it, Galen was the only passenger. Once again, he wondered how the Mer got around the Colony. Did they use water-filled aircars, or did they stay in their aquatic habitat, avoiding the rest of the population? He hoped it was the second choice. Allie had pointed out different Titan races to him when they met for dinner in the evenings, and he now prided himself on being able to identify at least a dozen. She'd never pointed out a Mer, though, for which he was glad, because he wasn't sure he could hide his disgust at a species that killed so indiscriminately. Because Halcyon couldn't have been acting alone. She had to have had help, allies, maybe a whole Mer army to create the kind of body count she was responsible for. Galen still found it hard to believe that only one Mer had taken down a ship the size of the *Poseidon*. She must have had a team of them then, just like she'd have a team of them now. Someone to help her sneak onto the ship. Someone who knew its inner workings so she could blow it up. Someone who constructed the bomb for her in the first place, because he knew there was no way he could have built one underwater, and no siren could beat him when it came to Human technology.

Of course, he'd done everything alone, but he was Human, capable of walking around in the air and working in precisely the right place to make and plant whatever he needed to. No Mer could do what he could. Not to mention he'd have noticed the moment one entered his workshop. He wouldn't need Allie to point them out – he'd smell them coming.

Not that there would be any Mer in the maintenance corridors beneath their dome, Galen thought with considerable relief as he palmed open the door to the restricted area. Only authorised personnel had access. A terrorist like Halcyon would probably bribe her way in, or threaten someone into giving her illegal access. At least, that's what he'd say if anyone asked him how she'd gotten in.

The sound of gushing water echoed through the corridors as the hatch crunched shut behind him. If he closed his eyes, Galen could almost imagine himself at sea in a lifeboat again, wishing for rescue in whatever form it came. Then, he'd even hoped the siren he'd seen would help him. Thank the universe she'd ignored his pleas for help and swum away, if she'd even heard them. Galen wasn't sure he could have lived with himself, knowing he owed his life to Halcyon.

He shoved through the memories and strode into the bowels of the Colony. Tonight he'd lay his trap to catch a siren, and soon he'd spring it. His parents' shades could rest, knowing they'd been avenged.

After what felt like forever, he emerged into the main pumping station. The spring erupted in a fountain in the middle of the cavern-like space, filling the room almost to the level of the catwalk where Galen stood. A labyrinth of pipework ringed the room, drawing water from the spewing source and carrying it ever onward and upward to supply the Colony.

Galen knew exactly where he wanted to place his package. There was a spot where a dozen inlet pipes converged, and something as small as a new water purification unit...or a nuclear device masquerading as one...might go unnoticed.

He still had an hour before the lights dimmed and the Colony's night began, though, so it was possible that someone could walk in on him. Unlikely, but possible. Galen took the uranium rods out of his toolkit, and nearly dropped them, they were so hot. He managed to stash them out of sight under the steps, hoping they wouldn't melt the metal before he transferred them over to the bomb. He had to work quickly, then.

He stripped down and donned a wetsuit, then perched on the edge of the catwalk to wedge his feet into a pair of fins. Galen left his toolbox open on the edge of the catwalk, within reach of the water, and slid into the depths. He bobbed on the surface for a moment as he adjusted his rebreather mask, tapping it until the lights glowed into life, before he submerged completely.

Underwater was a completely different world. No wonder Mer seemed so alien to him – they didn't even breathe air, or so he'd been told. He'd never gotten close enough to see one's gills.

Galen swam carefully around the fountain, which sounded thunderous under the surface. Visibility was low with so much turbulence, but he knew if he kept to the walls, he'd be able to follow the pipes to the nest of inlets. The pump casing hindered him at first until it filled with water, and then it was just an extra weight to tow along until he reached the spot. Just like the schematics showed, there was a perfect little alcove between three pipes, just big enough to fit the pump casing, but shadowed by the pipes overhead so it wouldn't be immediately visible. Plus, when it blew, the bomb would damage at least ten pipes within the blast radius of the explosives alone. It was a shame to destroy such an ingenious water supply station, but his team would be the ones rebuilding, so they'd soon get it back in working order, secure in the knowledge that no terrorist would target it again.

Galen had planned to fasten the casing in

place, but it fitted so snugly in its alcove that it wasn't necessary. Nothing but the blast itself or a seriously strong water current would budge it. Now all he had to do was pop the payload in and he could be home before dark.

He kicked off the side of a pipe, but his fin caught on the join, so it was wrenched off his foot. Cursing, Galen reached for it, but in vain – his fin sank into the depths, deeper than he could go with just a rebreather. It didn't matter. There were plenty more where those had come from – dozens to spare in the equipment store at the end of the catwalk. He peeled off the other fin and set off in the direction of the steps.

It was harder going without his fins, especially now he was fighting the current, too. He felt the faint pull of the pipe inlets as he passed them, but that was actually a good thing, as it kept him away from the fountain. He made it halfway back before a particularly strong tug dragged him upward, into one of the pipes closer to the surface. Galen tried to fight it, but the current was too strong, pulling him along until his shoulders wedged into the pipe and he found himself stuck fast.

He fought to free himself, but the suction of a pump somewhere above him was stronger than any pressure he could exert, plus the water pouring into the pipe behind him, rushing to reach its destination, pushed him deeper in.

His rebreather only allowed him an hour of air. Past that, and he'd drown. He had to calm down and think. If he was wedged too tightly in the pipe to get himself out, he'd need help. He couldn't call anyone, so the next best thing was to trigger an emergency alert. The easiest way to do that was to block the pipe, and hope there was still someone up to answer the alert before his air ran out.

Galen spread out his arms and legs, trying to angle his body so no water could get past him. The current buffeted his back, trying to force its way through, but he held fast, fighting to block the flow for as long as his strength held out. His only hope was to trigger an alert.

After an eternity that was probably no more than fifteen minutes, Galen gave up. He hurt all over and the pressure was starting to make his head pound. Or maybe he was running out of air. He hoped it had been enough.

Something brushed his bare foot. Something warmer than the water. Galen twisted his head to try and see behind him. His headlight reflected off something orange, before he saw nothing but water. It couldn't be. He blinked, watching the pipe inlet again.

This time, he clearly saw a coppery tail fluke brush against his foot, before the rust-coloured Mer blocked off the end of the pipe.

Halcyon. It had to be. Galen tried desperately to squeeze inside the pipe so she wouldn't see him, but all he succeeding in doing was to bash his head so hard against it that he saw stars. Then the stars faded to blackness. Galen's last memory was terror at what the siren would do to him – a helpless Human caught in her world – before he lost consciousness altogether.

THIRTEEN

"If we were Human, they'd have done something by now. It's because we're Titans that we're being ignored," Sven grumbled. "You're the only one who listens."

"I'm sure that's not true. I heard he's been testing the water all week, trying to find your mystery contaminants. There's nothing, Sven. I'll pull up the results myself, just to show you." Allie extracted her tablet, swiped at it a few times, then held it out to the frowning merman. "See? The springs supplying the Aqua Dome are some of the purest in the Colony. What kind of results are you getting in the aquaculture tanks? If there's a problem, it could be in the pipes, or the tanks themselves. There's so many things that can go wrong between the source and your fish."

"What do you take me for? No one knows water quality better than Mer. We can smell it. But our test results are just as mysterious as yours. They show nothing. But the fish…I've never seen anything like it. Nor have any of the others."

"Show me, then," Allie said. "If we can't find your problem in the water, maybe the answer lies with your fish."

She followed Sven along the raised catwalk between the pools, watching his muscles ripple and flex as he undulated along the surface. His tail was quite a striking shade of green, brighter than it really needed to be right now. Sven was showing off, she realised.

He dived under a section of catwalk and

came up in the middle of a pool teeming with fish. Huge fish, bigger than anything they'd brought into the Colony. Nothing grew this fast in the space of a few weeks, unless…

"What do you think?" Sven waved at the school circling him. "They're fully mature and the flesh is just superb. We harvested a few when they reached minimum size, but this is more than we can eat. We could supply the whole dome for a month from this pond alone. We'll have to, because at this rate of growth, they'll be sexually mature within a month and we'll be overrun."

"If you have that much to spare, send a few fillets my way. I can't remember the last time I had fresh tuna," Allie said, staring at the tank. It was a lie. The last time had been with her husband, before the war. He'd been working on accelerated growth as a recessive trait, so the population could build up rapidly before he'd released a spawning of fish without the acceleration gene. Within two generations, he'd had a sustainable population with a normal growth rate. "Where did you get these fish?"

"The fertilised embryos from Ceyx' lab," Sven admitted. "I know you don't like to hear his name, and I've heard stories about how you two met and fell in love. They've been embroidered into legends, to listen to the young mermaids sighing about you two like some sort of fairytale. But that was so long ago. Surely it's time to move on." He wiggled his tail suggestively.

Allie shook her head. "It's not that. He should be remembered. His work, as well as who he was. He'd have been thrilled to see his project doing so well. I only wish he'd lived to see it." She stared at the fish, avoiding Sven's eyes. "In the short term, I think you should deal with the oversupply by sharing it with the rest of the population. There's a vacancy for a seafood supply shop in Metropolis. I know a lot of the restaurant owners would love to have access to some of your fish. If you apply for premises tonight, I can slot you in for fitout tomorrow. You could be selling tuna fillets to Humans before the week's out."

"I'll look into it," Sven said. "But only if you promise to consider…there are other mermen here, eligible ones right here in the Colony. Not all of us supported the neutrality the Mer Council decreed. Some of us watched your victories with admiration. Any one of us would be both willing and capable of giving you children when you want them. You only have to ask."

To someone unfamiliar with Mer society, Sven's offer wouldn't sound the slightest bit romantic. But once you understood the nuances of Mer mating, where the females tended to rule while the males took care of children in between their other duties, it took on a whole new light. If she allowed a merman to give her a child, he'd dedicate himself to being her lover for as long as it took to conceive the child. After the birth, he'd care for it until it reached adulthood, for two or perhaps even three decades. Sven was offering something akin to a Human marriage proposal.

And for all the love she'd shared with Ceyx, she'd never carried a child past the first trimester. He'd assured her it was neither his genes nor hers that were the problem, but a combination of the two. Allie had all but given up on children long before Ceyx died. Now…just thinking about it brought back memories of her many miscarriages. And threatened to break her heart anew. She refused to lose anyone else.

"Thanks, but no," Allie said abruptly. "You said you'd planned to start another tank of tuna. If you fill the pond now, I could better observe their progress, because I'd be here at the start."

"Yes, ma'am," Sven said. He swam up to the control board. "I'll fill pools twelve and thirteen. Twelve will have embryos from Ceyx' stock, while thirteen will use unmodified stock from the colony ship, so we can see the difference." He turned the valve, muscles rippling again.

Water fountained up in a pool to Allie's left.

"You've got good water pressure here. I remember seeing something about the powerful flow rate in the springs, but I didn't think I'd be able to see the difference between this dome and the others. It must be because you're closer to the source." Within minutes, the pool was full, and the one beside it began to fill up. When it was perhaps a third full, the outlet started to sputter before the flow stopped altogether. "Ooh, that's not good."

Sven frowned. "It's never done that before." He leaped over the catwalk into the next series of pools to investigate. "It's still flowing, but it's down to a trickle," he reported.

"Maybe the pump died," Allie said, reaching for her tablet. "Col, show me all the error reports for the Aqua Dome water supply for the last six hours." There was only one – a blockage in the pipes, down near the supply source. "I better go down and fix it. I shouldn't take long."

"It'll be nightfall before you get there. Go home. Fix it tomorrow, and come back when you're ready. The embryos can wait another day. Get some rest."

Allie nodded and called for a skimmer, but she didn't tell it to go home. Instead, she directed it to the maintenance corridors beneath the dome, not even getting off the vehicle to palm open the door. She was soon whizzing down the corridors as the roar of the fountain drowned out all other sound. Glad to let the skimmer steer itself, she tried to call Galen, to tell him about the blockage, but he didn't answer.

Maybe the man was finally getting some sleep, instead of working late like he usually did. She would, soon, too, just as soon as she'd fixed this.

Allie was surprised to find a toolbox and a set of Maintenance coveralls already in the pumping station, but the owner of them was nowhere in sight. Probably already fixing the problem, she reassured herself. She checked the toolbox lid, and her mouth fell open when she recognised it was Galen's. He was the boss;

unblocking pipes wasn't his job. And the clothes were cool to the touch, like he'd been in the water a while. That wasn't good at all.

Fearing the worst, Allie stripped out of her coverall. If she was wrong, she'd head home to bed and leave the job to Galen. If she was right…oh, please, don't let her be right, she begged the universe. If she was right, Galen could be running out of air and stuck in a pipe. If he hadn't run out of air already…

Without hesitation, Allie dived into the water.

FOURTEEN

"Hey, boss? Remind me to show you the pool tomorrow. There's a NO SWIMMING sign on the wall here for a reason."

Galen's head hurt and he was freezing. Oh, and his arms burned, from the shoulder right down to his elbows.

"Wasn't swimming," he managed to say. His brain raced, trying to work out how to explain this to Allie. He settled for, "There's a bomb in there. I tried to get to it, but…"

"Yeah, I found it," Allie said. "That's not all I found, either. Someone tried to blow up the Colony. You interrupted them, and it nearly cost you your life. If it weren't for you, we'd all be dead."

No. That wasn't right. Galen hadn't planted enough explosives to damage more than the space in this room. Halcyon must have done something. "How?" he asked.

Allie pointed at the uranium rods, nestled in some black fabric that looked suspiciously like his wetsuit. "There's enough plutonium there to blow this place twice over. The bomb was a distraction; nothing more. If even one of those rods hit the water, this whole Colony would be nothing but a crater. You must have scared the saboteur away before he could finish the job."

Not he. She. Galen sat up, then wished he hadn't, because the pounding in his head increased in intensity. He flopped back down. No wonder he was cold – he was lying naked on the catwalk. What must Allie think? The shrinkage alone… "Where's my clothes?" he mumbled.

"Your clothes are right where you left them, over there." Allie pointed. "Your wetsuit…well, it tore while I was trying to get you unstuck, so I helped things along a little until I managed to get the wetsuit off you altogether. I might have scraped off a bit of skin getting you out of the pipe, but I wasn't sure how much air you had. I figured you'd forgive me a few grazes as long as I got you out before you ran out of air."

She'd saved him. How, he didn't know, but right now, he didn't care. "Thank you." The heartfelt words just didn't seem like enough. He'd have to think of a way to thank her properly. She'd taken such a risk. If she'd come here while Halcyon was still here, Allie would have been killed like he almost had been. Numbly, Galen pulled on his pants, then his shirt. His hands shook as he struggled with the buttons, but he didn't dare ask Allie for help. She'd done so much already, and she'd nearly…she'd nearly…he'd nearly lost her.

Galen sank to his knees, breathing hard. He wasn't cut out for this sort of thing. He'd never killed anyone in his life. And to think that his attempt to catch the siren so he could keep Allie safe had almost killed her…it made him too dizzy to stand.

"I've dismantled the bomb," Allie said. "The explosives are relatively inert without the detonator. We should still take them back to the Watch as evidence, though. The plutonium is another matter. That's much too dangerous to leave here, but I'll need some sort of shielding for it. The wetsuit's just so I can touch it. That stuff is hot."

Galen pointed a shaking finger at the pump casing. "Take the explosives out of that and put the…what did you say it was?" Uranium. He'd been certain it was uranium. That's what nuclear bombs were made out of, back on Earth.

"Plutonium. The result of the decay of radioactive uranium. Powerful source of alpha radiation with a very long half-life, which is what makes it so dangerous. Especially in water." Allie dumped the explosives into Galen's tool box and bundled the wetsuit with its radioactive contents into the pump casing.

"How do you know that?" Galen asked.

Allie shrugged. "Experience. There was still a supply of plutonium batteries aboard the Human spaceship when they came to the system, and they've been used to power transportation modules. Especially those attempting to be stealthy and operate without engines. Submarines in particular. The easiest way to check if a battery was still good was to measure the temperature. If it was hot, great. If not, the nuclear fuel was spent and it was safe to dispose of."

"But….batteries. Not enough to make much of an explosion, right?" Galen couldn't take his gaze off the pump casing now he knew what it held.

'I already told you. There's more than twice what you'd need to blow this place up. Just one of those would be more than critical mass, under the right conditions, like the ones here. That's why we can't leave it here." Allie shoved the box of explosives into his arms. "Here, you take this and your toolkit. I'll take the payload. I've already called for an aircar that'll be waiting for us when we leave the maintenance corridor, but we'll have to take a skimmer from here. Unless you'd rather walk?"

Galen quailed under her searching gaze. He wasn't sure his legs would hold him. He'd built a nuclear bomb. A bomb big enough to take out the entire Colony and all its inhabitants. He shook his head, trying to dislodge the thought, but it was stuck firmly in his mind. He'd never killed anyone, but he'd nearly killed everyone. To take out one terrorist.

If he'd succeeded, he'd have been worse than Halcyon. Killed more people. Done more damage.

Numbly, he climbed up behind Allie on the skimmer, oblivious to his surroundings. When she took him to the Watch, he'd confess everything. Someone like him should be locked up, where he couldn't hurt anyone. Allie should never have rescued him. She should have left him to drown in the pipe like he deserved.

Genocidal maniac. Mass murderer. Terrorist of the worst kind. Not Halcyon. Him.

FIFTEEN

By the time they reached the aircar, Galen had sunk into a deep state of shock. He didn't respond to a word Allie said and she had to half carry him into the aircar, where he curled up on the floor in the corner with his back to the wall, looking like a stricken elf who'd drunk so much moonshine he couldn't tell the difference between his own hallucinations and reality.

The man could do with a shot of

moonshine, Allie decided, as she loaded their gear into the aircar.

Her first thought was to take Galen to his apartment where he could sleep off his shock, while she reported to Ira with the dismantled nuclear weapon, but the man was a wreck. He shouldn't be left alone in his current state. Especially not if the person who'd planted the bomb recognised him and came after him at his apartment.

No, Allie decided, she'd take Galen to her place instead. There was space for two, so she could stay with him, and she was more than a match for any Human who managed to follow them to her apartment. Any Titan, too, but most Titans knew that, so they wouldn't try something that stupid. Besides, the bomb had all the hallmarks of Human technology, not Titan, especially the plutonium payload. The canisters that held the radioactive material were battery casings, for goodness' sake.

She had to tell Ira, but she needed Galen to tell him what he knew, too. And right now, the man wasn't coherent. Ira could wait until tomorrow. As long as she kept the evidence close where no one else could touch it, it would keep until morning. Galen needed her now.

She left the box and the pump casing just inside the doorway of her apartment before returning to the aircar for Galen and his things. He moved like an automaton, or someone who'd been subject to Titan mind control. Surely that wasn't possible, though. A Titan and a human teaming up…it was unheard of. Not to mention no Titan would be stupid enough to blow up the dome where Mer lived. Unless one of the Mer was involved…but few Mer knew Human technology the way she did. If the Mer had managed to get control over Galen, though…

Once he'd shuffled into her apartment and taken a seat on her couch, Allie asked, "Galen, was there a siren in the tunnels with you today? Did she give you orders?"

Even as the words left her lips, Allie didn't

believe them. For all Sven's talk of support, mermen lacked the voice range to use a song to control anyone, Human or Titan. And no mermaid would dabble with explosives. None of this made sense.

"I saw her," Galen said grimly. "Because of me, she could have blown us all up. You shouldn't have saved me. Should have left me to drown."

Now Galen wasn't making any sense.

Allie narrowed her eyes, and really looked at him. He was still shaking, and his clothes stuck to him like he'd still been wet when he put them on, or the clothes had been damp from the fountain spray, or he'd broken out in a cold sweat since dressing. She laid a hand on his arm, and was surprised to find his skin colder than hers. No wonder he was shivering. She'd put her money on the man simply being in shock, nothing more.

She knew how to handle shock. "Let's get you out of those clothes and into bed," she said.

Any normal man's eyes would light up at that invitation. Even Galen's, on any normal night. Tonight, his gaze remained unfocussed and dull. It broke her heart.

"Here." She pulled him to his feet, not bothering to hide her greater-than-Human strength from him. He wouldn't notice. Allie made short work of his shirt buttons, shucking off his shirt more gently than she might have if this encounter had been motivated more by passion than pity. One day, when he was more himself, she would rip his clothes off and have her way with him, she decided. For a man who spent most of his day in a workshop, he sure had some muscle to show for it. Maybe it was moving all those heavy things around, or maybe he spent all his recreational time in the gym. She ran her hands down his chest, telling herself she was checking his core body temperature, while also satisfying her curiosity about the firmness of him.

"Ohh, Allie," he moaned. It was all the warning she got before he grabbed her and kissed her.

Slow and sensual, he made her breath catch in her throat with a kiss that was everything she could have hoped or asked for. If she'd known Galen could kiss like this, she'd have demanded a demonstration on the night they met, instead of running from it.

He broke the kiss, because she didn't want to. "My turn," he said.

"Your turn?"

He nodded. "You undressed me, so I should undress you."

Nudity had never bothered her before, but this was different somehow. This was a man who'd never seen her naked before. And who wanted to do more than just look at her naked body, she was certain. Allie swallowed. "It's been a long time since anyone but my husband has touched me like that," she said. Ten years. Ten long, lonely years. More than enough mourning.

Galen stepped away from her and bowed his head. "I'm sorry. I didn't mean to go so fast. If you're not ready for this…if the wounds are still too raw…"

Sweet man. Misguided, but still sweet. Allie shook her head. "Oh, I'm ready. I want this. I think even Ceyx would wish me happiness, if he could. I'm just…rusty, is all."

Galen grinned. "Now, that's where you got lucky. Working in Maintenance, I know just how to get rid of all the rust, and rub you up until you feel all shiny and new."

Allie laughed. "Been practicing that line, have you? Is that the first time you've used it?"

"I've rehearsed it so many times in my head, what I'd say and what I'd do if you ever gave me the chance to make love to you," Galen admitted. "I'm still not certain if this is a fantasy or if it's real."

"It's real," Allie promised him. "But I'm all for a bit of erotic fantasy."

Now their clothes couldn't come off fast enough. Allie pulled Galen toward the bed, luring him with kisses as the logical part of her mind reminded her that she had to keep him warm. They'd barely touched the sheets before he was inside her, filling her to the hilt with all the wonderful sensations she'd missed, and a few new ones that she suspected were unique to Galen.

Ceyx had known her all her life, but he'd never given her pleasure the way Galen did now. So much for the Mer being legendary lovers – she could feel the evidence of Human superiority with every powerful thrust into her depths. They fit together so perfectly it was hard to believe they were two separate bodies and not one, so attuned to one another that at the peak of her pleasure, her cries of joy echoed his.

When they were thoroughly sated, she lay in his arms, staring at the Milky Way stretching across her skylight. Her body felt akin to the sky, for in one night Galen had ripped away her loneliness and filled her with so much more than she'd ever expected that it felt like she, too, was made of a million stars. She could hear her own heartbeat, the thrumming rhythm nothing but the tempo behind the song humming through her blood.

A siren song indeed. One she had no intention of resisting.

SIXTEEN

Galen awoke bathed in starlight, lying a bed where he held a beautiful naked woman in his arms. If he'd died and there was indeed an afterlife, he wasn't sure he deserved one this perfect.

Allie's eyes blinked open. "Oh, good, you're awake. It seemed rude to jump you while you were still asleep." Before Galen could say a word, she threw a leg over his hips and guided him inside her. "Stars, that feels so good," she moaned, grinding against him.

Entranced, Galen let her take charge, content to watch pure pleasure lighting up her face. He'd never met a woman so wild and free and joyful. And he wanted her to stay that way. Free of pain and suffering and fear. He'd do anything to protect her. Anything to make her happy. He held on as long as he could, wishing she could dance on top of him like this forever, but she was too caring a lover to pay attention to only her own pleasure. She soon had him gasping her name, meeting every rock of her hips with a thrust of his own, until he swore by the stars that he'd never felt anything as good, either.

He thought the fun would be over for a little while, as they both had to work today, but when Allie pulled him into the shower to help her clean up, as she put it, he soon forgot about anything except the flow of water, the slide of wet skin on skin and the way she turned his world upside down when she brought her wicked mouth into the mix.

Much later, when he reluctantly dressed, Galen's plan was clear in his mind once more. Yesterday he'd made a mistake, one which had almost resulted in tragic consequences, but that very fact made it even more important that he blame the whole mess on Halcyon. The Watch could hunt her down, catch her and imprison her somewhere where she couldn't hurt anyone ever again. Once she was caught, Allie would be safe, and he could spend the rest of his life making her happy.

Maybe she'd even let him move into her apartment here. It was definitely the bigger of the two, and he wondered how she'd managed to qualify for such a nice place, with a window, no less, when she was just a Maintenance worker and he was her boss, but he didn't have this kind of luxury.

Allie flashed him a joyful smile then, filling his thoughts with visions of her from last night and this morning. He had no space for silly suspicions. He was utterly, irretrievably in love with her, and he didn't care about anything else.

SEVENTEEN

Allie sent Ira a short message, telling him she'd meet him in his office at eight in the morning, and she'd bring a witness to the attempted sabotage she'd found.

Galen was too busy hunting through her refrigerator for breakfast to notice. "Where's all the food?" he asked. "There's nothing in here but ration bars and a tiny block of chocolate."

"Chocolate?" Allie immediately perked up.

She was certain she'd eaten the last of it a week ago, and she had yet to find a chocolate shop in the Colony that could satisfy her craving for the Human confection.

"Chocolate is not a breakfast food," Galen said. With a frown, he added, "And nor are ration bars, unless you're starving and there's nothing else."

Allie wisely decided not to tell him that she'd eaten nothing else for most of her time in the Colony. Cooking was not her forte, and while the Mer had promised her a shipment of fresh fish, it hadn't arrived yet. The only meals she'd eaten that weren't survival rations were the ones she'd shared with Galen.

"Maybe we can pick something up from one of the tea or coffee houses on our way to meet with the Watch. I'm sure some of them serve breakfast," she said.

"The Watch?" Galen looked nervous.

Allie was perfectly calm. "Of course. We need to get this evidence into the right hands, where it will be safe. I don't want to keep explosives or nuclear fuel in my apartment. That sort of thing is dangerous."

She summoned an aircar and they were soon zipping through the corridors of the Colony to Ira's office.

"I thought we were going to the Watch," Galen said. "Isn't this…?"

"Metropolis Central, where the master controls for the entire Colony are, and the head of the Watch lives?" Allie smiled. "Indeed it is. For something this serious, I figured we'd go straight to the top."

Galen looked like he wanted to argue, so Allie pushed the bundle of bomb parts into his arms and marched him to the door of Ira's apartment. She was five minutes early, but she had yet to see him in any other state than fully dressed and ready for work. Allie knocked briskly on the door, opened it, and led the way in to Ira's home office.

She dumped the wadded-up wetsuit on Ira's desk and gestured for Galen to do the same with his burden.

"What's this?" Ira asked, poking the wetsuit. Heat from the plutonium had melted it together in places so the canisters were almost completely concealed.

"The makings of a nuclear bomb. In fact, when we found it late last night, it was almost operational. There's enough plutonium in there to destroy the Colony twice over." Allie swallowed as her eyes met Ira's ice-blue ones. "You were right. There are people who would destroy the fragile peace we've created here."

"Plutonium? Only Humans use that, though quite rarely now, as most of it is spent. In fact, the only remaining stocks we're aware of are in the hands of the Humans First terrorists." Ira flicked a glance at Galen.

Allie didn't miss the way Galen stiffened, either.

"It's not only Humans who use it," Galen said. "The siren Halcyon has set off radioactive devices on at least four occasions, starting with the sinking of the *Poseidon*."

Allie stared at him, not sure what to say to

that.

Ira was not similarly constrained. "That's not common knowledge. Where did you hear that?"

"I was there. Only one person survived the *Poseidon*: me. I managed to get away in a lifeboat before the siren sank her, and when the ship blew up, I was far enough away that all I had to contend with were the waves. I didn't know the explosion was nuclear until the investigation team told me later when they tested my blood for radiation poisoning. I'd asked them to retrieve my parents' bodies when they refloated the ship. The poor guy had to explain to me that there weren't any bodies, as there was barely any ship left to salvage."

Ira and Allie exchanged a glance, but said nothing.

Galen continued, "If you know about the *Poseidon*, then you know she killed plenty of others during the war. She targeted Human ships, destroying them all in the same way.

More people escaped from the later ones, though, so there were plenty of witnesses. And now she's here, trying to destroy the Colony."

"Why do you believe that?" Ira asked.

"It represents peace between Titans and Humans – something she's dead set against. I'm surprised she didn't try to attack the peace talks, but maybe those were too well guarded, so she decided to target this place instead. At first, I thought it was only a rumour that she was in the Colony, but last night confirmed it. I know she's here because I saw her. I'd remember that rusty tail anywhere. She trapped me underwater and if it wasn't for Allie here, I'd be dead," Galen said.

Allie swallowed, trying to moisten her dry mouth. "She was present throughout the peace talks. Halcyon was the Titans' chosen mediator. If she hadn't been there, none of the Titan delegation would have attended. There would be no peace, and the Colony wouldn't exist. Since that time, she's been one of the strongest Titan voices for peace."

Galen snorted. "That's complete stardust. She blew up at least six buildings on Elysium after the peace treaty was signed. All places where both Humans and Titans worked in the same building. She's so pissed off the war ended that she's taken to killing her own people now, too."

"All the attacks on Elysium have been traced back to Humans First activists," Ira said. "There is no mention of Halcyon or in fact any Titan in the official reports. All of the suicide bombers on those occasions were Human."

Galen paled, but his expression grew stony. "I know what I heard, and I know what I saw last night. She was there. Find her, and interrogate her. See what she has to say for herself."

Ira steepled his fingers together. "Perhaps we will. In the meantime, can you recount the events of last night, please?" He set his tablet on the desk, tapping the screen so that it would record Galen's testimony.

Ira listened for a long time, just nodding his

head, before Galen ran out of breath. Then Ira had a few questions, just asking him to clarify things he'd said, before he dismissed Galen.

Allie rose to leave, too, but Ira held up his hand. "Stay. I need to speak to you, too," Ira said.

Galen looked torn, like he wanted to stay with Allie but he really, really wanted to get away from Ira. "I'll get you some breakfast, and a coffee, okay? I'll wait for you," he said finally, backing out of the room.

Allie waited until the door had closed behind Galen and his footsteps had faded away. She took a deep breath. "No, he doesn't know. No Human does."

Ira turned his x-ray stare on Allie. "Did you do it?"

"Like you need to ask. The bomb's been made by an amateur, not a professional. Someone who's never made one before, or trying to make it look that way. If it weren't for the plutonium, and the location, I wouldn't have bothered you. And for the record, all four of those ships blew because of poor Human engineering. All I did was sink them. Water, the pressure, and poor storage practices for the nuclear submarine batteries did the rest." Allie waved at the display on the desk. "If this had been my work, the Colony would be dust right now, and we wouldn't be standing here."

Ira nodded. He knew her well enough to know she wouldn't bother blowing stardust up his butt. "Is it possible that another Mer…?"

"No. No one else would dare. They wouldn't defy the Council, and any who would…well, then there's me." Allie thought of Galen's strange behaviour last night. Shock or mind control? She still wasn't sure.

Ira read the doubt in her expression as if he'd read her mind. Perhaps he could. Allie still wasn't certain which Titan race he belonged to, but she had nothing to hide from him. However, if he rummaged too far into her head, he'd stumble across her memories of her bed play with Galen. She almost wanted him to find them, so she could see his expression when he did.

"I want you to speak to the Mer. Make certain it wasn't them. I'll assign some Watch officers to the investigation, and let you know what I find in the surveillance footage." He eyed the mess on his desk. "I take it it's too much to ask for you to take this with you?"

Allie shook her head. "I think you need to keep it safe. The plutonium alone…and what if there's more? I'll ask Col to search the Colony. It might help us find the culprit, but it'll definitely make this place safer." She raised her voice to issue an order to the AI.

It was Ira's turn to shake his head. "You know you're the only person in the entire Colony who talks to the AI, don't you?"

Allie shrugged. "It's intelligent and it obeys orders. Much like any Human or Titan under the control of a siren song. Force of habit, I guess." She rose. "Are we done? If I know Galen, he'll have found something lovely for breakfast and it'll be getting cold. If the Watch find anything useful on the surveillance footage, let Violet know. She'll inform me."

"You're subverting my staff now?"

"Not yet. I don't need to. We're working toward the same goal. I understand you're too busy to keep me informed about everything, so I took the initiative." Allie winked. "In case you're interested, her weakness is chocolate, and I'm sure she'd appreciate some for a job well done. So would I, if you find a good supplier in the Colony. I've run out." She turned and strode out of the office, leaving Ira grumbling under his breath. Allie hid her smile. It was shaping up to be another beautiful day.

EIGHTEEN

Galen made it back to the entrance to the Watch building just as Allie stepped outside. Her beaming smile as she spotted him warmed his heart. He had done the right thing up in Ira's office, he told himself. Protecting her was worth any price.

"I brought you a muffin," he said, holding up the bag. Actually, he'd bought half a dozen, but he'd eaten a couple along the way to quiet his roaring belly.

Any other girl would have asked what kind, or reached for the bag to find out. Allie reached for his hand instead and said, "Let's go somewhere a little more private for breakfast. How about the park in the middle of the Arbor Dome?"

Galen was only too happy to agree. Within moments, they mounted a skimmer and the acceleration as it took off pressed her sweet body against his, making his breath catch in his throat. After last night, he never wanted to be separated from her again.

Allie let the skimmer carry them deep between the trees before she leaped to the ground. Galen followed more slowly, trying not to spill the coffee. The skimmer zipped off and out of sight, leaving them alone in the forest.

Allie let out a blissful sigh. "Much more peaceful than Metropolis. Let's sit here." She pointed at a bench, artfully placed on the edge of a clearing filled mostly with a pool of crystal-clear water. It looked like something out of an old Earth painting. It probably was, Galen realised, seeing as someone had created this, just like everything else in the Colony.

They both sat. He passed Allie her coffee before he ripped open the bag containing their breakfast.

Allie clapped her hands. "Oh, you're an absolute sweetheart, Galen. Chocolate muffins. I think I'm in love." The kiss she gave him in return confirmed it.

A crazy idea popped into his head. One he couldn't seem to dismiss. He barely knew her and they'd kissed for the first time barely a day ago, but he already knew he wanted to spend the rest of his life with her. And life could be so short, with war and terrorists and who knew what else around the corner. That's why he had to ask her. Had to…

Galen opened his mouth to give voice to his heart's most ardent proposal.

"Galen, I need to tell you something. Something I should have told you before," Allie began.

Galen closed his mouth and signalled for her to continue.

"While you were telling Ira about last night, I realised that – "

A raucous bark of laughter interrupted her, followed by several others.

"Ooh, lovebirds in the forest."

"A pair of Humans."

"Don't they know it's dangerous in the woods?"

Four men emerged from the shadows, all of them barefoot. They prowled forward, more like animals than men.

"Shifters," Allie said softly. "Hunters of some sort. I'd say wolves, but I don't think so. More likely some sort of cat."

"Get in the water, then," Galen said urgently, rising to his feet. "Cats don't like water. I'll fend them off while you call for help."

"Tigers like water just fine," one of the men growled, stepping forward. "And it'll only take one of us to hold you down so you can watch how the rest of us entertain your little girlfriend. This is our territory, and you're trespassing, Human. Your kind need to be taught a lesson."

Allie burst out laughing. "A bit too melodramatic before breakfast, don't you think, boys? This is public land, free to be enjoyed by all Colony residents. At least, those who have the social skills to stay." She lifted her coffee from the seat beside her and sipped it before she started to hum a cheerful song Galen didn't recognise.

"Leave her alone," Galen said through gritted teeth, squaring up for a fight. He'd learned in the college dorms that his age and size made him a target, so he'd made it his mission to learn how to defend himself. Four Human opponents was the most he'd ever had to deal with, and even then he'd come out with a couple of broken ribs and a black eye, but it had been worth it. He hoped Titans weren't harder to fight than teenage boys high on hormones and adrenaline. If only his brain didn't feel so fuzzy. Should have had more sleep last night. "Run, Allie," he pleaded.

Allie stopped humming. "Hi, I'm Allie, and this is my friend, Galen." She gave a little wave. Galen caught a glimpse of something orange like a flame between her fingers before it disappeared. He must have imagined it. "We're responsible for your water supply in the Colony. When there's trouble, I come along to your house and sort things out. I'm very good at what I do, right, Galen?" He found himself nodding. Allie continued, "I enjoy my work, too. I like to sing while I'm working. I find it makes everything better."

The shifters met Allie's spiel with silence. It jarred with the voice in Galen's head telling him to run or fight, but that voice seemed to grow fainter even as he tried to focus on it.

The man at the very back gave a little salute. "You enjoy your breakfast, ma'am." He and his fellows melted away into the trees.

Galen shook his head, trying to fight the fog that filled it. "Allie? What just happened?"

None of it made sense.

Allie's hand grasped his arm and pulled him to sit beside her again. "Just making friends with the neighbours," she said. She reached for a muffin and bit into it. "Mm, this is wonderful. You're going to have to tell me where you got them."

Galen sighed and grabbed a muffin. The moment was gone, stolen by a bunch of shifters. He couldn't ask her now, or the memory of his proposal would be forever tainted. Another time. At dinner, perhaps. When he wasn't feeling so foggy.

At his side, Allie began to hum softly again, and the world was wonderful once more.

NINETEEN

Allie was making her final adjustments on the fitout for Seafood Supply, Sven's new fish shop, when she received an incoming message. Violet wanted to meet her for lunch at a café on the other side of Metropolis. Allie fired off a quick affirmative before she started to pack her tools.

"Are you finished already?" Sven echoed the response of almost every satisfied customer Allie had dealt with.

"I used to fix Ceyx' fish tanks on the ship. I could have done these ones in my sleep," she said.

"When do you want your fish? I can grab them from the cool room now, if you like. You forgot them last night."

Was it only last night that Sven had flirted with her and promised her fresh fish? It felt like so much longer.

"How about I swing by after work this evening, if that's all right? At the Aqua Dome, not here. I want to ask you something," Allie said.

A slow smile spread across Sven's face and he winked. "Whatever my lady wishes."

Allie almost corrected his mistaken assumption, but decided it didn't matter. Maybe she should bring Galen along tonight, just to stir things up a little. And if a siren truly had been messing with Galen's head, perhaps she'd give herself away with some spark of surprise – or Galen might recognise her.

She waved goodbye to Sven and took a

skimmer to see Violet.

The moment Allie stepped off the skimmer, she had to take a deep breath. The most exquisite sweetness, wrapping a core of earthy bitterness assailed her nose. Chocolate. Fresh and hot and…

Violet waved to get Allie's attention. "I found you a chocolate shop. What do you think?"

It wasn't just a shop. It was a café whose menu consisted solely of cocoa-based products. It truly was a wonderful day, Allie said to herself as she followed Violet inside.

"We'll have two orders of the chocolate chili and…what would you like to drink?" Violet said, turning to Allie. "I hope you don't mind me ordering, but I heard from a dragon that their chocolate chili is the best he's ever tasted. One of the Watch fire mages swears by it, too."

Allie smiled. "Whatever you recommend. I'm still growing accustomed to Human food, and I like to try everything at least once."

Violet finished ordering for them and led the way to a secluded corner table. As she settled in her chair, she asked, "What do your kind normally eat? I mean, you all kept to yourselves so much on the ship. I never saw any of you in the messhall. I never really thought…"

Allie waited for the waiter to fill their water glasses, then drank deeply to give the Human waiter time to get out of earshot before she answered, "Fresh fish, when we can get it. Lately, it's been a mix of ration bars and a selection from eating houses as they open. The other Mer finally have the aquaculture farm up and running, so they'll be selling fresh seafood tomorrow, I believe. I'll get my order in advance, of course."

"Of course." Violet nodded. "How do you cook it? I mean, on land, you'd use a normal kitchen like the rest of us, but in the water…"

"We don't. Cooking removes many essential nutrients and destroys the fresh texture. I believe Humans do something similar, though they call it sashimi."

Violet looked horrified. "Raw fish? Remind me not to date a Mer. Present company excepted, of course."

Allie inclined her head, accepting the oblique apology. "Do you have any information for me?"

Violet nodded and pulled out her tablet. "My boss asked me to investigate the surveillance footage for a particular maintenance tunnel. It was all rather urgent, and he pulled me off another investigation so I could do this today. All I heard was that someone had planted a bomb, and they wanted to know who had the opportunity. I combed every surveillance camera for that corridor, the maintenance tunnels, everything. And all I found was two people. You, and this guy." She tapped the screen, then tilted it so Allie could see. "He looks familiar. I'm sure I know him from somewhere."

Allie watched Galen struggle with his toolbox and what looked like a residential water pump as he palmed the door open and disappeared inside. Her heart sank as she recognised the pump as identical to the casing that had housed the bomb. It couldn't be Galen. Or if it was, he had to be under someone else's control. He wasn't a killer. There was just no way he'd blow up the Colony. It was a suicide mission, and he was smart enough to know that. The Galen she knew didn't have a death wish.

Someone had definitely mind controlled him, she decided. That was the only explanation. And when she found out who…she'd tear the siren's tits off.

TWENTY

Fear curdled in Galen's belly as he approached the Aqua Dome. Now he was so close to his decade-long goal, he was terrified. It didn't help that Halcyon had starred in all his nightmares since the ship sank. She'd ripped away everyone he loved, and he couldn't let it happen again. His arms tightened around Allie's waist as the skimmer raced through the corridors to the Mer habitat.

"They prefer communal living to individual

apartments," Allie said over her shoulder. "So their habitat is different to most. They manage the aquaculture facility that supplies the whole Colony with seafood, or it will when their fish stocks reach harvestable size. It's early days yet. At the moment, all they're producing stays within the Mer habitat. They only eat the freshest seafood."

Galen couldn't believe what he was hearing. "Fish who eat fish? Isn't that cannibalism?"

Allie laughed. "Back on Earth, the bigger fish ate the little fish because that's all they had. It's not cannibalism when they're different species, and it's the same with Mer. Mer have more in common with Humans than with fish. They're marine mammals, after all. Didn't Earth have marine mammals? Dolphins, and something bigger, too?"

"I've seen pictures of dolphins. They weren't much bigger than a Human, but they spent their whole lives in the ocean. There are tales of even bigger things – whales, my mother called them – that were the size of a ship, but I find that hard to believe. How could something so huge survive? What would it eat?"

"Whales sound intriguing. I hope there's DNA stored in the databanks somewhere, so one day scientists can create them again and they'll swim in Altan seas," Allie said dreamily.

Galen suppressed a snort. Here he was, terrified of coming face to face with the woman who'd killed his parents, yet knowing he owed it to his parents to seek revenge if he could. All the while, Allie was talking about monsters even more frightening than the murderous Mer, and how much she wanted to meet them. If she met Halcyon, she'd probably want to shake hands with the woman, or whatever Mers did. It was as though Allie had been born without a sense of fear.

Dangerous. No wonder he wanted to protect her so much. She did so little to protect herself. Wanting to meet monsters indeed.

"We're here." One moment she was in his

arms, the next she bounced down off the skimmer, holding out a hand as if to help him down. "C'mon. What are you afraid of?"

"Halcyon," he blurted out.

Sympathy filled her eyes, or perhaps it was pity. "Mers are pacifists, and the ones here more so than most. You have nothing to fear from them, I promise. Halcyon is…unusual, even for a Mer. When she joined the war effort, it wasn't popular. She…let's just say you probably shouldn't mention that name around the Mer you meet today."

Galen nodded, wondering for the umpteenth time how she knew so much about Titans and the war. Perhaps she'd studied politics or modern history while he learned engineering, then switched to plumbing because all the political jobs were taken.

"Why did you become a plumber?" he asked.

Allie stared at him for a moment before she answered, "To get into the Colony, of course. I signed up as an apprentice in the construction phase, and volunteered as one of the Colony residents the moment they opened for applications. I knew this was where I needed to be, and here I am. Queen of the pipes." She laughed.

Did that then make him the king? If it meant a lifetime with her, he'd take the job in a heartbeat. This was hardly the time or the place to say so, though.

They entered a farming zone, which was made up of ponds as far as the eye could see, with narrow jetties between them.

"It's nearly dinnertime, so most of the Mer will be fishing. This is the best place to meet everyone. If you see anyone you recognise, let me know," Allie said.

Galen nodded, scanning the ponds for signs of life. What he'd taken for still pools were actually teeming with fish, and a surprising number of brightly-coloured Mer. Blue and green, gold and silver, black and white…so many shades, but not a hint of orange among them. Slowly it dawned on him that Halcyon wasn't here. But if she wasn't…where was she? It wasn't like she had anywhere else to go. The only water habitat in the whole Colony was here.

"Is everyone here?" Galen asked Allie.

She shrugged. "I don't know. I'll ask Sven." She waved at a group of men entering the farming zone. One of the men finished pulling off his shirt and waved back.

The whole group headed in their direction, led by a shirtless dude showing off his six-pack. "My lady," the show-off said with an elaborate bow.

Allie shook her head. "Just Allie, please. Galen, this is Sven. Sven, Galen is an environmental engineer who's in charge of Maintenance for the Colony. He's the one who's been working on your water problem with the tuna tanks." She took a deep breath. "Galen, Sven is – "

"The Patriarch of the Green Line, and every mermaid's wet dream," Sven finished smoothly. He peeled off his pants and dived into the nearest pool. When he surfaced, the man had turned emerald green, from his head down to the tips of his tail flukes. "As you can see."

Galen couldn't seem to close his mouth. The man had turned into a mer…well, not a mermaid. A merman, maybe. If he had man parts under that tail somewhere. Maybe Mer really did spawn like fish.

The other men who'd arrived with Sven stripped and entered the water, too. They changed and surfaced, each a slightly different colour. Not all of them were the monochrome of Sven the show-off, though – most of the Mer were flesh-coloured above the waist, and only their tails took on a different hue. Including – Galen gulped – the women. Two of what he'd thought were men turned to face him in the water, their bare breasts on full display. He didn't know where to look, and if Allie caught him staring at some other woman's breasts…

"You missed all the fun, Allie," one of the

men said, emerging from the water with a handful of small fish. He lifted one wriggling fish high into the air, then swallowed it whole. "After you left, a trio of tiger shifters stumbled out of the bar and started picking fights with the Humans in the square. It turned into a brawl of about thirty people before the Watch broke it up. We might have to sell…what do Humans call it? Popcorn, that's it. We might have to start selling popcorn and seats for that sort of entertainment."

Allie frowned. "Why didn't you break it up?"

The man spread his arms wide. "Do I look like a siren? I don't calm mobs. If Humans and Titans want to fight, we won't interfere. Let the lesser beings fight out their frustrations with each other. Mer farm fish and keep their own counsel. If we're forced to watch as part of our participation in this community, fine. We'll bring snacks." He swallowed another fish, then dived under for more.

Allie let out an exasperated sigh. "Sven,

Galen wanted to know if everyone's here, or if anyone's missing."

Sven surveyed the pools. "No, this is everyone. Why, is he looking to mate with someone? One of the younger mermaids might be curious about getting with a Human. She might eat him alive, too. He's not exactly the bravest of them, is he? He nearly pissed himself when I changed."

He had not pissed himself. "I've never seen a man shapeshift into a fish before," Galen said stiffly. "I didn't know you could do that."

Sven grinned. "Humans know very little about the Mer, and with good reason. They'd know even less if it wasn't for…" He exchanged a pointed glance with Allie, who shook her head. "So you've never met a Mer before, or at least, you didn't think you had. You could have seen any of us walking around the Colony and not known we were Mer."

Could Mer read minds, too? Galen suppressed a shiver.

"Is there anyone you recognise, Galen?"

Allie asked.

"No," he said firmly. He'd never seen so many bare breasts in one place, and it was making him more than a little hot under the collar, plus a few other places, too. He didn't want to look too closely at the women. Especially not in front of Allie. None of them had an orange tail, which meant none of them was Halcyon. That meant she could be roaming anywhere in the Colony, looking for all the world like a normal woman. He didn't know what her face looked like, only her tail. He could have walked past her today and not recognised her. "We should go," he said urgently.

"All right," Allie said. She inclined her head to Sven. "Thank you. I should head home. It's been a long day."

Sven's face fell.

Galen felt an irresistible urge to grin at the merman's disappointment. Did the fish have a crush on Allie?

"Don't forget your fish," Sven said. "I'd

offer to deliver it to your apartment, but then I'd have to put clothes on." A few of the Mer within earshot laughed.

Someone climbed out of the water and returned with a cooler box that she handed to Allie.

"Thanks, Leukosia. You don't know how long it's been since I had fresh fish." Allie clutched the box to her chest.

Galen held out his arms. "Let me take that for you."

Allie surrendered the box, and one of the mermen muttered something in a language Galen didn't understand. Whatever he'd said, it didn't sound complimentary. Allie glared at him and gave him a one-fingered salute that evidently meant the same in Mer as it did in Human.

Galen waited until they'd reached the entrance to what he'd now think of as the Mer nudist colony before he said, "Did you understand what he said?"

Allie nodded grimly. "He said you were

insulting me, calling me weak by taking the box. He suggested I show my strength by…um, avenging the insult. With violence."

Galen stopped. "I figured they were making a joke at my expense. If I'd known…want me to go back there and sort him out?"

"I don't need you to fight my battles, Galen. Besides, they'd only say it was an even bigger insult. I'd have to do something to you then."

"I could never fight you," Galen said. "I'd be too scared I'd hurt you."

Allie smiled, but said nothing as she summoned an aircar. The box was too bulky for a skimmer.

"What are you going to do with all that fish?" Galen asked.

"Eat it, of course." She stared at him. "But not tonight. Let's drop this off at my place, then go out for dinner again. My treat."

"Last night you saved my life. I'm pretty sure I owe you a lifetime's worth of dinners for that," Galen began, seeing his opportunity.

"That depends. How good are you at

cleaning and gutting fish?" Allie asked, laughing, as she boarded the aircar. The aircar was crowded, so he had to sit on the other side from her, where his proposal once again went unsaid. At dinner, he promised himself, or afterwards. Then he'd ask her for forever.

TWENTY ONE

All through dinner, Allie fought to find the fortitude to tell Galen who she really was. She wasn't afraid of his reaction. She'd seen hatred in countless Human eyes before, just because they knew she was a Titan. It's just that last night had been the most pleasurable night in her memory, and she didn't want to hurt him. Was one more night with him too much to ask? It wasn't like he'd hate her any more in the morning than if she told him now.

When the waiter delivered dessert, Galen clasped his hands together on the table and said, "Allie, I need to ask you something important."

She already knew what it would be, but silently she begged the universe for one more night.

Allie set down her spoon, then held up both hands to stop him. "What with everything that happened last night and today, I'm not sure I can take any more. The only thing I want to do tonight is to climb into bed with you and spend the whole night believing there's no one else in the universe but us, and the most important thing in life is for us to see as many stars as possible."

Galen's jaw dropped. "And by stars you mean…?"

Allie blushed and stared down at her plate. "All the times I screamed your name last night, it was because you made me see stars."

"I'd like to give you every star in the sky, Allie," he said, his eyes starting to smoulder.

They paid the bill and called for a skimmer. Galen's arms wrapped around Allie as he stepped up behind her, and she pushed back against him, grinding her bottom against his crotch until he was so hard that his pants were probably feeling uncomfortably tight.

"Stars, Allie. If you keep doing that, I might have to lay you down right here on this skimmer," Galen groaned in her ear.

Allie laughed softly as she pressed against him again. "I'm pretty sure there's a law against that."

"I don't care."

Yes, this was the right thing to do, she thought as the skimmer pulled up outside her apartment. They made it inside, but that's all the decorum they had time for. Before the hatch had completely slid shut behind them, Galen pinned her to the wall. A quick struggle loosened their pants enough to give him access and he plunged deep inside her to the tune of matching moans from both their throats.

Allie wrapped her legs around his hips,

drawing him deeper still. Yes, this was exactly what she wanted. Galen's powerful lovemaking with all the wild abandon she'd never known from anyone else. Her first orgasm took her by surprise, though not Galen, judging by the way he chuckled when she cried out.

"Enough stars for you, sweetheart?" he asked, slowing his pace but not stopping.

"So many," she sighed blissfully. "But I want more."

"Then I'm taking you to bed." Strong hands cupped her bottom, holding him inside her as he carried her to the bed. Galen sat down, so that Allie sat in his lap.

She unfastened her legs from around him and tugged her pants all the way off. He'd lost his pants somewhere along the way, so now it was skin on skin as she knelt astride him, clenching hard at the burning heat he still held between her thighs.

"I need to taste your breasts," he said, peeling off her shirt. "I saw all those mergirls with their tits out and the only thing I could think of was how much I wanted yours."

Allie laughed. "If I'd been sitting naked in that pool, I'm sure you wouldn't have looked twice at me, not with all those women to choose from."

"If I saw you naked in that pool, I'd have stripped off and joined you. No matter how many Mer were watching." Galen seized her hips, and spoke slowly so that each word matched his thrusts, "I love you, Allie. I only want you. Forever."

Tears sprang to her eyes. Not since Ceyx had anyone ever…

Allie screamed as her second orgasm engulfed her. She couldn't stop the tears now. But she could give him stars. A whole galaxy to match the pleasure he gave her. She grasped his shoulders, rocking her hips as she rode him hard, letting her core clamp down on him as she felt her third climax building, bigger than the first two. As big as the man inside her, giving her so much more than she'd ever hoped for.

"Oh, fuck. Stars, Allie!" he shouted as he reached his peak, barely a moment before she hit hers.

"I love you, too, Galen," she murmured, kissing his neck.

And that was why tomorrow would be terrible but tonight...tonight the universe existed for them alone, so they could share all the stars.

TWENTY TWO

Galen didn't want to get out of bed. Allie had woken him twice in the middle of the night to make love, and the way she was stirring now, she might be about to ask again. She didn't need to ask. Galen let his fingers trail across her breast, down her side and across her belly to her thigh. "Good morning, sweetheart," he whispered as he slid the tip of his finger inside her, stroking gently.

"Mm." She snuggled closer to him. "I hope

you're planning on using more than just one finger to wake me up."

"Two?" He demonstrated.

"Think harder, Galen. And bigger. Oh, yes!"

One very enjoyable hour later, Galen had to admit they needed to get up or they'd be late for work. If this was life with Allie, it was better than anything he could have imagined. He'd do anything to keep it that way.

Allie's comm beeped just as he was getting into the shower, so she reluctantly left him to shower alone to take the call. She still wasn't back when Galen was clean, so he turned off the water and headed out to the living area in a towel to see what had kept her.

"Check again, Col," she said, her eyes darting from her tablet to the wall screen, which both showed schematics of the Colony.

"What are you looking for?" Galen asked.

"Something that's not there, Col says, which is not possible, seeing as it was before. I have time to sort this before my first fitout this morning, but I might head out to the spots where it's found an anomaly, just to make sure." Allie frowned at the screen.

"Want me to bring you breakfast?" he asked.

She waved him away. "I'll be fine. I'll pick up something on the way. Today's not going to be as nice as yesterday. Meet you for dinner, maybe?"

"It's a date," Galen replied, kissing her cheek. He wanted more – so much more – but he was already late, so he hurried into his clothes and headed out. He could ask her tonight.

When he reached his office, a box half hidden under his desk caught his eye. It was a pump box – the one that still held the other half of the plutonium. He couldn't believe he'd just left it lying here like this, but he'd thought it was uranium, and not enough to cause trouble. Now he knew better, he just wanted it gone.

Galen heaved the box onto the desk and opened it. He took a deep breath before he lifted the lid of the lead-lined box inside. Sure enough, two rods remained, and they were hot to the touch. It was enough to blow up the entire Colony, Allie had said, so that meant these leftovers were just as dangerous. It needed to be locked away where no one would find it and use it.

The Watch had presumably done that with the first two rods, so they must have a suitable storage facility. He'd tell them one of the staff had found it in one of the other main pumping stations. Arbor Dome, maybe. Let the Watch draw whatever conclusions they liked from that.

Then he was done. Done building bombs; done trying to track down terrorists; done with the hunt and everything to do with that bloody siren Halcyon.

Because he didn't want to draw her attention to himself, as that would only put Allie at risk. He'd give up anything to protect Allie, because she was his future. His parents would understand, he was sure. They'd want him to be happy. And if killing Halcyon risked letting something bad happen to Allie…he'd never forgive himself.

His parents were gone, and nothing could bring them back. But Allie was living, breathing hope, and all he had left.

Galen dropped onto his chair, borne down by the sheer enormity of his decision. No more revenge. No more hunting for Halcyon. He'd have to find a hobby.

Feeling lighter, he pulled his music player out of his desk drawer and slipped the headphones over his ears. He turned up the volume and found himself singing along as he read through his morning messages. Nothing could budge his good mood today.

TWENTY THREE

Allie's communications chip told her she had an incoming message from Col about the AI's radiation scan. Not wanting to bother Galen with it, she headed for the living room so she could put the map up on the wall screen.

"How many locations?" Allie asked, pulling on some pants.

"Four point sources, plus three travel paths," the AI replied.

"Where is it now?" She clipped her bra.

"Unknown. No current radiation signatures match the profile."

Allie swore. That didn't make sense. Unless the plutonium was well shielded. Maybe their amateur was only pretending not to know what he or she was doing.

"Show me all the locations," she commanded, reaching for her shirt.

Half the Colony lit up. Three spots in Metropolis, plus one in the Aqua Dome, and a blue beam connecting them all and the route to Ira's office.

"Remove the travel routes," she said, savagely twisting the buttons as she fastened her shirt.

The beams vanished, leaving four blue blotches. "Zoom in to the site in Metropolis."

Allie blinked as the overlapping blotches separated into three different sites within the Maintenance building. A storage room, the workshop, and…no, that couldn't be right.

"Check again, Col," she ordered.

Her heart beat faster at the sight of Galen

wearing nothing but a low-slung towel, but she fought to ignore it. She'd love to take him back to bed and not have to go to work, but this was too important. She'd planned on telling him the truth this morning anyway, so it was time to steel her heart against the inevitable rejection she'd suffer when he found out about her past. First, she had to find the remaining plutonium and ensure the safety of the Colony. Then she could hand him her heart so he could blow it to bits.

She almost broke her resolve when he kissed her cheek. It would have been so easy to turn her head and offer him her lips instead. She forced herself to focus on the screen, though it showed nothing of interest right now.

Allie didn't allow herself to relax until the hatch had slid shut behind Galen, sealing him out of her life. While the AI completed its scan, she reached into the refrigerator for a snack. Sven had given her enough fish for a week, and her mouth watered at the thought. It had taken almost all of her self control last night not to strip off and join the other Mer as they caught their dinner fresh, but Galen would never have understood. And she'd wanted one more night with him…so the small sacrifice had been worth it.

The scan still wasn't finished, so Allie reached for another fillet. It sure beat ration bars.

"Scan complete. Additional source identified," the AI said.

"Where? Show me."

Allie's heart contracted in her chest as the map showed her the Maintenance building again. "Show me the building in 3D, as it is now."

"Additional source has disappeared."

Allie swore. "Show me where it was."

A blinking blue light appeared, almost directly on top of another spot dated several weeks previously. Allie was afraid to ask, so she looked for the other sites next. One was in a supply room, and the other was in the workshop. The radiation source in the supply room had sat there for weeks, since before the Colony was inhabited. Whoever had planted it had to have been on the construction crew, or it had arrived with the supplies. The workshop had seen a radiation source several times over the weeks they'd lived in the Colony. Whoever had carried it there was definitely a resident.

"Show me radioactivity in brightness levels," she said.

The spot in the Aqua Dome dimmed to about half what the others were. All except the additional source Col had found today.

She couldn't avoid it any longer. Weeks ago, before the source had moved to the workshop, it had sat in one spot, almost exactly where it had briefly sat today. It shouldn't be possible, but Allie had to believe it was. Whoever had built the original bomb had only taken half of their plutonium to the Aqua Dome. And they still had the remainder, ready to blow this place sky high on a whim. She wouldn't let that happen.

Allie summoned a skimmer and climbed numbly onto the footboard. She missed the warm, solid feel of Galen standing behind her, but she needed to forget all that now. Forget her feelings, forget everything she loved about him, and focus on what was important.

It was far too short a trip to the Maintenance building in the bowels of Metropolis, but Allie told herself it was for the best. Logic told her she should call the Watch for backup, but she dismissed that idea. She could handle one man on her own. Once she'd found out what she needed to know, THEN the Watch could have him.

She strode into the building with a confidence she didn't feel, not today. She didn't slow until she reached the entrance to the office she was after. Then, she paused in the open doorway, wishing she was wrong, but knowing she wasn't.

"Why did you do it?" she asked.

No answer. Galen kept his eyes on the screen in front of him, ignoring her.

"I asked you why you did it. I saved your life. I have a right to know."

His lips moved, and he started singing faintly. Still he ignored her.

Allie noticed his peculiar ear coverings, with which he somehow blocked out all sound, including her voice. That's how he'd survived the *Poseidon*. He'd never heard her song, never fallen asleep like the other passengers, which is why he'd made it to the lifeboat when the alarms sounded, because he had heard those. She should have sunk the lifeboat while she had the chance, all those years ago.

"Allie!" With a practised motion, Galen pulled his headphones down so they circled his neck. His smile died as he took in the tears streaming down her face. "What's wrong, sweetheart?"

She was not sweet. Allie surveyed the desk. Where the blue spots had glowed, now she saw only a box for a residential pump. The same sort of pump she'd found hollowed out and full of explosives in the Aqua Dome main pumping station. "It's in here, isn't it?" She reached for the box.

So did Galen, but she was faster.

"Don't, sweetheart. It's dangerous. One of the other guys found it in the Arbor Dome main pumping station, where – "

"Don't lie to me." She lifted the box lid, and felt a surge of triumph as she saw another box, and not a pump, inside. She opened the box, peering in just long enough to confirm that she was right, before she threw the whole thing back on Galen's desk. "I had to see it for myself, or I wouldn't have believed it. I saved your life. I helped you. I stood up for you against the Watch, when they would have…not that it matters now. I can admit when I'm wrong. When I've been so stupid, so blinded, by the man I thought was my friend."

Galen stared at her. "I am your friend. More than that, if you'll let me. Allie, I – "

"I don't want to hear it," she snapped. "All I want to know is why. Why you did it."

Still he stared, as if he didn't understand.

"You planted that bomb in the pumping station. You built it. You nearly nuked the whole Colony with all of us in it. I want to know why."

"I…" Galen swallowed. "It was an accident."

Allie snorted. "Stardust."

"It was!" he insisted. "I built the bomb, sure, and I planted it. I only took half the plutonium because I thought it was uranium, and I wouldn't have enough for it to reach critical mass. I calculated the explosive charge perfectly. It would have damaged the pumping station, but left the dome structurally sound, and contaminated it with enough radiation to make it look like she did it."

"Like who did it?" Allie demanded.

"Halcyon. The siren who killed my parents, sank the *Poseidon* and murdered thousands of other people."

Allie bit her lip. "Fifteen hundred and sixty-two. Not thousands. And every single one of those was killed in an act of war. They were not civilians."

"She murdered more than a thousand people. Including my parents. They deserve justice."

Allie shook her head. "It's not murder when military personnel are killed in battle. Even if it was, the peace treaty signed by both Humans and Titans declared a general amnesty so no one on either side could be accused of war crimes once the treaty was signed. Anyone who killed or tortured was absolved of their guilt, so that all the atrocities would stop. It was the price we had to pay for peace."

"Not me. I didn't choose it. I wasn't the only one, either. The Humans First organisation offered to help me find her."

"They're nothing but a bunch of suicide bombers, and the racist bigots who recruit and arm them. They wanted you to blow yourself up with thousands of innocent civilians, and you nearly did." Tears formed in Allie's eyes again. "You almost destroyed all chance of peace between our peoples, and for what? One woman?"

Galen wet his lips. "Allie, I – "

"Then take your shot, Human." Allie threw her arms wide. "Your search is over and no one else needs to die. Enough people have been hurt. I lost the man I loved and gained a psychotic stalker. Where's the justice in that?"

She took pity on Galen's confusion. "I'm Halcyon. I killed all those people, including your father, Doctor Claudius Tasker, the man who lured my husband into a trap by promising to share his scientific findings, then tortured him to death before my eyes. He deserved to die, so I made sure he did. And crazed with grief, a siren's grief, which you can't even begin to understand, I sang his funeral dirge. A song that drove whoever heard it to die. Your music machine saved you, so you never knew what killed them. Every Titan knows what a siren is capable of, which is why they don't harm us. That's why the Mer are all pacifists, serving as mediators in a conflict because if Mer fight, only they will

win. We know that, so we abstain. We tried —
the Mer Council decreed that we'd take no part
in the war — but Humans didn't listen. They
captured my husband and tortured him for
information. When they attacked him, they
attacked all the Mer. So my people gave me
permission to retrieve him, or seek justice as I
saw fit."

Allie sucked in a deep breath, swiping at her
tears. Now was not the time.

"I saw the torture chambers. Ceyx was killed
in one, but there were many others, and they
all showed signs of use. Prisoners were kept on
Human ships and interrogated under torture
before they were killed. I saw the mutilated
bodies, and made sure their tormentors
suffered. So I knew, when we declared that
amnesty, that I had at least brought some to
justice. I came to realise that the only way to
stop Humans from torturing Titans was to
either kill them all or end the war, and to that
end, I agreed to mediate the treaty. I am the
only living Mer to have gone to war, and

Titans remember the stories. They know who and what I am, and they fear me because of it. It's only Humans like you who think I need something as crude as a weapon to destroy this place. I am a living weapon, but I will not be used against my people.

"So kill me now, if you must. I will die for the sake of peace, to keep you from killing anyone else. I'm no innocent. I have the blood of hundreds on my hands. There is no one left who loves me enough to mourn me, and the Mer have sworn they will not avenge me. So kill me."

Still Galen stared at her. "Allie, I…Halcyon." He swallowed. "I can't."

TWENTY FOUR

Allie – Halcyon – waved at the box on the desk. "Fine. Be a coward. But if you use that to kill all the people in the Colony instead, you'll be a worse man than your father ever was. You'll be sealing the fate of your entire species, because the remaining sirens will not let such a deed go unpunished. I'm ashamed to think I considered you a friend. You are what you call us – monsters." She turned on her heel and stalked out of his office. Perhaps even out of his life.

"Allie, wait. Please," he begged, but she didn't return. Why would she? She was right. He was horrified at the thought that he'd nearly detonated a nuclear weapon here, in a city full of civilians. With children, for stars' sake. It was small comfort to know that he hadn't killed anyone. He'd planned it, and come so close to executing that plan that it was a miracle the Colony was still standing.

Saved by Halcyon. She'd saved him and the city. And he loved her, because she was Allie.

Though she had every right to hate him.

Galen buried his head in his hands. He hated himself.

He wasn't sure how much later it was when the Watch came for him. Minutes, maybe even hours, but he wasn't aware of the passage of time. Only the crushing weight of guilt that he knew he deserved.

"Mr Galen Tasker?" a female voice asked.

"Yes." The word came out as a barely audible whisper. Galen didn't want to be himself right now. Not ever.

"You're under arrest for possession of a weapon of mass destruction. I'm to request you come with us willingly, or we'll press additional charges for acts of terrorism, resisting arrest..." she continued in the same vein for a little while, but Galen wasn't listening any more.

He didn't care. He deserved everything he got for what he'd done, and for what he'd almost done. The universe would be safer with him locked away where he couldn't hurt anyone again.

Galen rose to his feet and held out his arms for handcuffs. The things his mind could imagine and his hands could build...better if both were restrained. He only wished there were a way to turn his brain off, too, so he no longer felt or thought.

"Bring the box," the woman in charge ordered to one of her underlings as she and another Watch officer seized Galen's arms to march him outside to a waiting aircar. "And be careful with it," she called over her shoulder.

Galen kept his head down, not caring where they took him. It was either a holding cell or a shuttle off-planet. When they reached the Watch building, his escort guided him left instead of right, toward the offices belonging to high-ranking members of the Watch, as opposed to the cellblock. Perhaps the interrogation rooms were this way, Galen told himself. Or maybe they had torture chambers like his father once had, and they kept them close to the offices so the bigwigs didn't have as far to walk to get their sadistic urges satisfied.

If he survived the torture, or even if he didn't, he should try and get a note to Allie, telling her about it so she could deal with those who did it. Maybe the universe would be a better place with Halcyon loose. His life had been.

"Don't know what you're smiling about," the Watchwoman muttered, tugging on Galen's arm to keep him walking.

Her companion opened a door at the end of the corridor and pushed Galen inside.

"Mr Tasker, sir," the woman said before she shut the door behind Galen, leaving him alone with…

Ira, the man in charge of the Watch, and the whole Colony, or so Galen had been told.

"Take a seat, Mr Tasker." Ira gestured to one of the chairs in front of his desk. Identical chairs to the ones where Galen had sat with Allie when he'd tried to frame her for his own stupidity.

Galen shook his head. "I prefer to stand."

"Suit yourself. I take it you know why you're here."

Galen started to shake his head, but another Watch officer stepped into the room, dropped the incriminating box on Ira's desk, and left. Galen sagged. He might not know exactly why he was here, but he had a damn good idea.

Ira began, "One Halcyon Mavros, an undercover Watch operative whose cover is her role as Colony plumber, initiated a search for radiation leaks. This morning, she reported several in the region of your office, Mr Tasker. When she investigated further, she found not just a radiation source, but what she identified as a weapon of mass destruction. On your desk."

"Does Halcyon really work for you?" Galen blurted out. "How do you know she's not just pretending to work for you while she'd biding her time, to pursue her own agenda?" What if everything she'd said and done with him had been a lie to seduce information out of him?

"Ms Mavros is not a patient woman, Mr Tasker, but she is an honest one. Perhaps a little too honest at times. I've worked with her since before the treaty was signed. Long enough to know that she will pursue her own agenda, no matter what you want her to do, and the only way to make sure she's following my plan is to make sure it shares the same goals as hers." Ira coughed. "If she says pigs are falling from the sky, then I would advise looking out the window, because you'll see a remarkable sight."

Galen's eyes darted to the window, but there weren't any pigs to see.

"I was speaking figuratively, of course," Ira added, his eyes glinting with amusement.

"So if she talked about people torturing prisoners…" Galen began, unsure how to finish.

"Then prisoners were tortured."

Galen wet his lips. "And her husband? Seeks, I think she said his name was?"

"Ceyx, yes," Ira said. "He was captured by Humans and tortured for information. The chief interrogator assigned to him was Claudius Tasker. Your father, I believe."

"She definitely killed him? And fifteen hundred…more than fifteen hundred other people?"

Ira frowned. "That number does seem high. Much higher than my estimates, but I imagine she'd know. If you asked her, she could probably tell you the names of each and every one of them."

Galen shook his head. "I don't think she wants to talk to me any more. Not after what I did."

Ira folded his hands on the table. "Tell me, Mr Tasker. What exactly did you do? Not the version you gave me last time. The truth, please."

So Galen told him everything, from his first contact with Humans First, finding the nuclear fuel they'd smuggled into the Colony, building and planting the bomb, right up until he arrived in Ira's office today. It felt good to get everything out in the open. After all, what did he have left to lose? Nothing.

The only thing he didn't talk about was his personal time with Allie. That was…private. Glorious. And none of his blasted business.

As if the man had read his mind, Ira asked, "So what are your current intentions toward Ms Mavros?"

His intentions? He'd wanted to marry the woman. Galen wanted to go back in time a few hours, to when Allie was naked in his arms, and stay in bed. Forever. He wouldn't know she was a killer, and she wouldn't know he was an idiot, and everything would be perfect. If time travel were possible, he would, too.

"Is my operative in danger around you, Mr Tasker?"

Allie? Never. He couldn't hurt her. It didn't matter how many people she'd killed or who she was. She was still Allie. Galen couldn't live with himself if he hurt her. Even if she did hate him now.

"No. No, she's not," Galen said finally. "I don't intend to do anything with her, because I don't think she wants anything to do with me."

Ira nodded, glancing down at his tablet. "I have two choices here, Mr Tasker. I can ask you to repeat your confession so we can record it, as I seem to have forgotten to set up a recording device for our interview, and I can then have you shipped offworld for trial. Or, I could use your existing, recorded confession and that of Ms Mavros from earlier in the week, where she states her belief that your mind might have been in the control of another, such that your actions were not your own. If that were true, you might not need to be sent offworld at all. Your lesser offence would be under New Hope jurisdiction, which means I could sentence you to house arrest for a year. The likely terms would still allow you to live and work in the Colony, but when you leave your apartment, you would be escorted by a guard at all times."

"A year?" Galen expected a life sentence in prison if Ira sent him offworld. Why would his sentence here be so light?

"That could easily change, depending on your behaviour. Good behaviour might lessen your sentence, while any infractions, however small, could lengthen it considerably, or make me change my decision and send you offworld after all. I'll receive monthly behaviour reports, of course."

Galen still didn't understand. There had to be some darker purpose to keeping him here. His eyes strayed to the pump box of plutonium. "What will happen to that?"

"It will be stored somewhere safe. With the rest of the radioactive material," Ira replied. "Now, I'm a busy man, Mr Tasker. Do you wish to repeat your new testimony so it can be recorded, before you are taken offworld, or would you prefer to return home under house arrest?"

Like there was a choice to make. "I'll stay."

Ira nodded. "Your guard will be waiting outside." He dismissed Galen with a wave of his hand.

Galen opened the door and stopped dead at the sight in the corridor. "So that's it. You don't expect me to survive the year."

TWENTY FIVE

"You don't expect me to survive the year."

Allie wanted to cringe away from the hostility in Galen's eyes, but she forced her expression to remain neutral. Ira had made it clear that if Galen was to stay out of prison, she would have to be the one guarding him, because he wasn't about to allocate any of his other staff to such a menial assignment. Allie knew he wouldn't last five minutes in a prison. It wasn't like he'd killed anyone, and she truly didn't believe he would. She was willing to bet her life on it.

She was hurt that he thought so little of her that he believed she'd kill him, but she wasn't surprised. After all, he'd hated her for a decade, with good reason. Just because he'd slept with her when he'd thought she was someone else didn't mean he'd give up ten years of loathing. He probably hated her even more now for fooling him, however necessary it might have been.

"Have you changed your mind already, Mr Tasker?" Ira called.

Galen dropped his gaze to his handcuffed wrists. "No."

The door hissed shut behind him, leaving Galen alone in the corridor with Allie. He looked ready to bolt.

"I can take the handcuffs off now, if you like," she said, pressing her thumb to the scan panel. The cuffs clicked open. She was relieved to see Violet hadn't fastened them too tightly The cuffs had left no red marks on Galen's wrists. "Your ID chip is now coded to mine. You'll have to stay within a certain distance of me, or both the Watch and I will receive an alert. You can still go to work and you'll have some privacy, just…oh, and if Col spots you near an unusual radiation source, it'll notify me, too." She took in his slumped shoulders and the way he wouldn't look at her. "Would you rather go to prison?"

"Ask me in a month," he said bitterly. "His high and mightiness in there said it's still a possibility."

Not if she had any say in it, Allie vowed. Ira would get nothing but good reports about Galen, if she had to mind control the man herself to make him behave.

TWENTY SIX

For six weeks, Galen endured the conditions of his house arrest. The best and the worst part of it was Allie.

She wished him a good morning every day as she unlocked his apartment door to release him from captivity, walked him to work or worked alongside him if a maintenance job required two of them, and shared every meal with him in silence. At night, she wished him a good night before she locked him in and escaped to her own apartment, or a hot date, or whatever she chose to do with her freedom in the evenings.

More than once, he'd considered following her. He was an engineer, after all, and the door controls were hardly more complex than anything else he'd built. The only thing that stopped him was the thought of seeing her happy with someone else. He understood that she hated him now, seeing as she could barely stand to look at him, but he wasn't sure he could handle seeing the woman he loved in another man's arms. It was hard enough knowing he'd lost her through his own stupidity.

But it wasn't until they were working together on a bunch of blocked drains at the strip club that he noticed she wasn't singing any more. Allie had always sung or hummed something while she worked.

"Are you feeling all right?" he asked her.

"Of course not," she said. "I have yet to meet anyone who can keep their lunch down after they've unblocked three toilets in a brothel and the fourth one looks like…looks…ugh."

She did look distinctly green, he realised, but that went right along with doing a disgusting job. The dark circles under her eyes were new, though. He tried to remember if she'd looked like this yesterday. "Yesterday, you missed lunch. Today, you're throwing up. Plumbing aside, what's wrong?"

"Nothing that won't go away on its own," she said. "Look, can we just finish this job so we can go do something else that doesn't stink like someone died in here?'

Galen nodded and switched the pump back on, but he found his eyes straying to her more and more as the day progressed. She seemed listless and tired, like she'd never been before. When the day ended, he'd made up his mind.

"I'm sick of eating by myself at home every night. Want to go out for pizza?" he asked her.

The eyes she turned on him looked almost haunted, they were so hollow. "I'm not hungry, and it's been a really long day. I'll go with you to pick up a takeaway pizza if you want, but then I'm going home."

If that was the best she had to offer, he'd take it. She called for an aircar instead of a skimmer, so they wouldn't have to travel as closely together, he guessed, but when she sank onto the seat with a little sigh, he wondered if it was more about her exhaustion than anything to do with him at all.

Despite her protests, he ordered a pizza for her as well as the one for him, knowing the seafood one was her favourite. He carried the boxes back on his lap in the aircar, grinning as several of the other passengers cast covetous glances at their dinner. Just as long as it tempted Allie into staying with him for the evening.

They arrived back at his apartment and he palmed open the door. "You coming in to join me for dinner, or are you taking yours home with you?" he asked, hoping she'd choose him.

"I'm really not hungry," she began, then

clapped a hand to her mouth and bolted for his bathroom. Galen heard the sound of retching from behind the closed door.

He propped the pizza boxes open on his kitchen counter and grabbed two plates. He waited a few minutes for Allie to emerge from the bathroom, but when she didn't, he decided to eat a slice before it got cold. He could always reheat hers when she was ready.

He was three bites into his second slice when Allie staggered into the living area. She clutched at the doorjamb to stay upright and her face was paler than he'd ever seen it.

"You're not going anywhere like that. Come and sit down." Galen pointed at the dining chair across from him.

She almost made it, then stumbled as she reached the table. Galen grabbed her as she reached for him, and for the first time in weeks, he finally had her in his arms. He breathed in her scent — fresh, intoxicating and salty, like the sea, as always — and he almost moaned. He'd missed her so much.

"Let go of me. I'm fine," she said, grasping the table and hauling herself to her feet. She made it to her chair this time, but not without effort.

"You're not fine. Are you going to tell me what's wrong, or should I call a doctor?"

"Nothing's wrong!" she exploded. "Not yet, anyway. I'm pregnant, all right? This is normal."

Galen wanted to cry. She had moved on, finding some other man to seduce…no, some other Titan, he realised. It had to be, if the guy could get her knocked up.

"Whose is it?" he asked.

"Mine, for the moment," she said.

"I mean, who's the father?" Galen paused to think. "It was that green merman, wasn't it? I saw the way he looked at you. Like he wanted to cover you in cream and eat you."

"You mean Sven?" Allie snorted. "He wishes. He's had a crush on me since before he learned to turn his tail. He used to sneak off from the crèche to watch Ceyx and I, I'm sure of it. He might be a Patriarch now, but I remember when he was too small to swim."

"Who, then?" Galen persisted. He wanted to start an interspecies war with whoever the Titan man was.

"The only man I've slept with this year is you, Galen, so I'll give you one guess," Allie said. Before he could respond, she added, "Not that it matters. I can't carry a child to term. Five miscarriages have taught me that. Ceyx said it was the combination of his genes and mine, but I knew better. It was me. There's a reason no one else has a tail the colour of mine. Inbred is what I am, because the Mer community aboard our ship was so small, genetic diversity was damn near impossible. So I'll have to endure a few weeks more of morning sickness before I miscarry this one, too, in a wave of blood and pain. The universe never meant me to be a mother. I should have learned my lesson by now." She inhaled deeply. "You know, I think I will have some of that pizza. It smells really good."

Galen stared as Allie picked up a slice and took a huge bite.

Not sick. Pregnant. With his child. It wasn't possible.

"But we're different species. We can't breed," he said.

"Stardust. That's what they want you to think. Ceyx discovered we could and he died to protect his secret." Allie finished her slice of pizza and reached for another. "It doesn't matter, anyway. She won't live long enough to surface."

"You mean be born?"

Allie shook her head. "Surface. Cross-race Mer children are always female, born to swim. Mer give birth in the water, and the first thing she'll learn is to surface, closing her gills to breathe through her lungs. Later, she'll learn to turn her tail so she can walk like us."

Galen couldn't help laughing at the image that popped into his head. "You mean our daughter will be a mermaid?"

"Galen, don't get attached. In a few weeks —

"

Galen pressed a finger to her lips. "I'm not an expert in genetics, but you said your husband was. If you say his genes made you miscarry because you're too closely related, that doesn't mean mine will. In fact, a couple can't get more diverse than the two of us."

Allie didn't pull away this time, as his eyes held hers. "We're not a couple any more," she said. "You've made it abundantly clear that you hate me for what I did to your family."

"No, I haven't. You're the one who told me I was worse than my father because of what I nearly did to the city." Galen grasped her hands. "I don't care what you did in the past. I love you because of what you've done for me since I met you here. You've saved my life, stopped me from doing something incredibly stupid, and made every day I spend with you a pleasure. Even the ones where I don't get to sleep with you. I love you, Allie." He pressed a hand to her still-flat belly. "And I'm going to love her, too, when she's born. Even if she has a tail."

"But what if – "

"I'm going to take such good care of you, nothing will hurt this baby. I'll pay every credit I have to keep a doctor at your side round the clock until she's born." Galen swallowed. "If you'll let me. I mean, I'm under house arrest. I can't be with you every moment, even if I want to be."

For the first time in weeks, Allie actually smiled. "Actually, Ira never said it had to be your house you stayed in. You could come live with me. There's more than enough space for two at my place. Maybe even three, if she survives."

"She will," Galen swore. "I'll start building her a crib in the workshop tomorrow on my lunch break. What else will you need? Just tell me and I'll do it."

Allie blushed. "Actually, there's one thing that's different about this pregnancy. Something I never experienced before. When I'm not feeling ill, I crave sex like you wouldn't believe. Alone at night in my apartment, so many nights now, I imagined I was with you once more and…it's not the same, a poor shadow of the reality, but I want…you."

"I'm yours if you want me," Galen said. "Now and forever. Halcyon…Allie, I love you. Anything you want, you just have to ask."

"Stay with me, Galen. Sleep with me. Love me like…like I love you," she said.

"As my lady wishes," he replied. He hoisted her in his arms and carried her to his bed. As he set her on the mattress, Galen said, "You know, there's an old Human saying that would be perfect for us. Make love, not war."

Allie laughed and pulled off her shirt. "Yes, Galen. Make no more war. And love…it's such a strange phrase you Humans have. I never thought of love as something you can make. It's created, yes, but born out of so many things shared between two people. You make me feel love for you, and I want to…we would call it joining, where two people become one so completely it's hard to tell where one ends and the other begins. When you make love to me, there is only us, and a universe of stars."

TWENTY SEVEN

Galen crossed the aquaculture farm to the temporary apartment he shared with Allie until her time came. Any day now, the Mer doctor had said, and Allie had agreed. She looked ready to burst, and she'd taken to spending more time in the water than on land. He was fairly certain that's why the Watch had lifted his house arrest early. Not that he liked to be away from Allie for long, but when she got cravings for things, he'd scour Metropolis to get her what she needed.

Today it was chocolate, which he left on the counter in their empty apartment. She must be in one of the pools again, or in the Mer habitat proper, where they lived underwater. Allie had invited him in there a couple of times, giving him a rebreather so he could stay under for as long as she did, but he didn't feel comfortable in what he felt was nothing but a giant fish tank. Not to mention the Mer were a bunch of hippy nudists, which he wasn't sure he'd ever get used to.

Galen stripped down to a pair of board shorts. He wasn't ready to join the nudists, but he did want to sit with Allie in the water.

He spotted Leukosia as he passed the tuna pools. "Have you seen Allie?" he asked.

"Try the birthing pool," she said.

Allie had gone into labour already? Galen broke into a run.

The birthing pool was warm, wide and shallow, filled with Mer bodies of every colour. Every colour except orange.

"Where is she?" he asked urgently.

"I'm here," Allie's voice said, sounding strained.

Now he saw her – looking like a naked Human woman, not a mermaid, in the middle of the pool.

"She's coming, Galen," Allie cried, reaching for his hand as she gritted her teeth through a contraction.

The Mer women made space for him, and for once he didn't notice their nakedness. He had eyes only for Allie.

"She's crowning. Push again!" one of the Mer women said, peering intently between Allie's legs. She swished her tail impatiently. "Now. Push hard now!"

Allie screamed until she ran out of air, but still she pushed, panting for breath.

"Again!" the Mer doctor ordered.

Allie obeyed, but the look of agony on her face as she cried out to the stars above tore Galen's heart in two.

"You need to give her something for the

pain. Can't you see how much this is hurting her?" Galen demanded.

No one listened.

"One more!"

Allie squeezed Galen's had so hard he wanted to cry out, but he stayed strong for her. He had to.

"Oooh!" the surrounding crowd sang, as something small and rust-coloured shot between Allie's legs in a cloud of blood.

One of them caught the baby and brought her squirming to her mother's arms. Her tail made her look like a salmon, shimmery silver-pink, but her eyes were the colour of sage.

"Her name!" the Mer chanted. "What is her name?"

Galen ignored them, reaching to stroke his daughter's cheek. "She has my mother's eyes," he said softly, finding it hard to swallow.

"Then her name is Panacea," Allie said.

Galen knew he'd never told her his mother's name. Ira's words came back to him then — Allie might have killed hundreds of people during the war, but she knew every name. Allie was many things, but not a monster. And because of her, Panacea Tasker lived again, sired in the impossible union between two races that might one day learn to live in peace.

In the future, they would call times like these halcyon days, where peace reigned and no storm raged. For sometimes the universe needed a halcyon, a siren who could both call and calm the storm.

ABOUT THE AUTHOR

Demelza Carlton has always loved the ocean, but on her first snorkelling trip she found she was afraid of fish.

She has since swum with sea lions, sharks and sea cucumbers and stood on spray drenched cliffs over a seething sea as a seven-metre cyclonic swell surged in, shattering a shipwreck below.

Demelza now lives in Perth, Western Australia, the shark attack capital of the world.

The *Ocean's Gift* series was her first foray into fiction, followed by her suspense thriller *Nightmares* trilogy. She swears the *Mel Goes to Hell* series ambushed her on a crowded train and wouldn't leave her alone.

Want to know more? You can follow Demelza on Facebook, Twitter, YouTube or her website, Demelza Carlton's Place at:

www.demelzacarlton.com

Books by Demelza Carlton

Siren of Secrets series
Ocean's Secret (#1)
Ocean's Gift (#2)
Ocean's Infiltrator (#3)

Siren of War series
Ocean's Justice (#1)
Ocean's Widow (#2)
Ocean's Bride (#3)
Ocean's Rise (#4)
Ocean's War (#5)
How To Catch Crabs

Nightmares Trilogy
Nightmares of Caitlin Lockyer (#1)
Necessary Evil of Nathan Miller (#2)
Afterlife of Alana Miller (#3)

Mel Goes to Hell series
The Devil's Work (#1)
See You in Hell (#2)
Mel Goes to Hell (#3)
To Hell and Back (#4)
The Holiday From Hell (#5)
All Hell Breaks Loose (#6)
The Devil Goes to Heaven (#7)

The Colony: Aqua series

Halcyon (#1)
Poseidon (#2)
Apollo (#3)

Romance Island Resort series

Maid for the Rock Star (#1)
The Rock Star's Email Order Bride (#2)
The Rock Star's Virginity (#3)
The Rock Star and the Billionaire (#4)
The Rock Star Wants A Wife (#5)
The Rock Star's Wedding (#6)
Maid for the South Pole (#7)
Jailbird Bride (#8)

Romance a Medieval Fairytale series

Enchant: Beauty and the Beast Retold
Dance: Cinderella Retold
Fly: Goose Girl Retold
Revel: Twelve Dancing Princesses Retold
Silence: Little Mermaid Retold
Awaken: Sleeping Beauty Retold
Embellish: Brave Little Tailor Retold
Appease: Princess and the Pea Retold
Blow: Three Little Pigs Retold
Return: Hansel and Gretel Retold
Wish: Aladdin Retold
Melt: Snow Queen Retold
Spin: Rumpelstiltskin Retold
Kiss: Frog Prince Retold
Reflect: Snow White Retold
Roar: Goldilocks Retold
Cobble: Elves and the Shoemaker Retold

www.ingramcontent.com/pod-product-compliance
Lightning Source LLC
Chambersburg PA
CBHW070637170726
48291CB00003B/1046